A Gangster's Revenge

Aryanna

Lock Down Publications
Presents
A Gangster's Revenge
A Novel by *Aryanna*

Lock Down Publications
P.O. Box 1482
Pine Lake, Ga 30072-1482

First Edition September 2015
Printed in the United States of America
*This is a work of fiction. Names, characters, places, and incidents
either are products of the author's imagination or are used ficti-
tiously. Any similarity to actual events or locales or persons, living
or dead, is entirely coincidental.*

Lock Down Publications
Like our page on Facebook: Lock Down Publications
@www.facebook.com/lockdownpublications.ldp
Cover design and layout by: Jamie Lee
Book interior design by: Shawn Walker
Edited by: Lauren Burton

Acknowledgements

First and foremost, I want to give all my thanks to God because without him I'm nothing. I would like to thank all the positive and negative influences in my life because they taught me the delicate balance of power that makes up versatility. I would like to thank all my teachers who believed in me, nurtured my gifts and gave me the appreciation for education that I hope to pass along to my kids some day. I would like to thank my mother for showing me what a strong woman is and that you don't have to be perfect to embody that strength. I would like to thank all the people who matter to me. There's too many to name but you should already know who you are. I have to thank the streets of the DMV (DC,MD AND VA) for giving me the essence and not demanding my life to the cist for the game. I would especially like to thank everyone that played a part in this book. I am grateful and humbled for their help. I have to thank LDP for the family love, acceptance and opportunity they provided me. Its not always easy noticing or knowing what to do when you find that rose that grew from concrete. Thank you for believing in my dreams.

ARYANNA, I thank you for being born and bringing light into my life. You are everything I wanted and needed.

Lastly, I would like to give a special thanks to everyone who doubted me or believed all I would ever be is a pretty face. Thank you for always judging a book by its cover because now I'm on the cover of my own book. I did this shit and it's just the beginning.

LDP, The Game Is Ours.

Aryanna

Chapter 1

The Bells of Freedom

"See you around, Mitchell."

"Not on your life, motherfucker," I replied with a good-natured smirk and a firm middle finger salute as I strode out of the gates into the open arms of freedom. I didn't hear the CO's comeback, nor did I give a damn. I was out, I was finally out, and that meant I wasn't on anyone else's time except my own. I dropped my bag and took a moment to just admire the view of the unsettling, yet tranquil mountains in the distance. Unsettling because I'd been looking at those same sorry-ass mountains for the last four years of my sentence at Augusta Correctional Center. Today, this moment, was my last look, and that wasn't a promise. It was a guaranteed fact! I'd given the Virginia Department of Corrections twenty years of my life, and I refused to give them even one more, no matter what the cost or who had to pay it.

"Nigga, ain't you seen enough of these damn trees and the hillbillies that live in them?" she asked, eyes twinkling in the early morning sun with laughter and a hint of something livelier underneath. I gave her one of my seldom seen, but genuine smiles and scooped her off of her feet and into my arms.

"Boy, have I missed you, Light Skin," I said, kissing her with a loud smack on the mouth.

"I've missed you, too, Big Head. Now put me down so we can get the hell away from here." She didn't have to tell me twice as I sat her down, scooped up my bag, and strolled to the waiting car without a backward glance.

"Nice wheels for a college girl." I admired the 2021 E55 AMG Mercedes Benz.

"Well, you know, I do what I can, but it's time for an upgrade because this is last year's model."

"Damn, Kiara, is we getting it like that, yo?" I asked, running my fingers over the cherry-colored paint job.

"Big bro, you ain't name me Keyz for no reason." She opened the trunk so I could throw my bag in.

"Yeah, this shit fly. I thought shit would've been hovering by the time I got out of that muthafuckin' system."

"Don't trip, Big Head, you home now, and it's time to forget all that shit," she replied, pulling a black Samsonite suitcase from the trunk after I dropped my bag in.

Could I really forget what or who landed me there?

"Hello, earth to Devaughn!" Kiara said, waving her hand in my face. "I don't know where you just went, my nigga, but you need to stay out of those dark places. Shit, you scaring my girl."

I hadn't even noticed the badass light-skin chick exiting the car, but then again, it was impossible to see inside the car.

"Damn!" was all I could utter, looking at the gorgeous creature before me. She was no more than five feet, two inches with heels on and a body that screamed *fuck me*. The sun threw a blinding light off of the diamond dangling from her belly button, drawing my attention to her flat stomach and the tattooed tiger claws gripping her sides. I could tell she had a nice, juicy ass just looking at her from the front. Add to that her perfect breasts, long red-tipped dreadlocks and hazel eyes, and you had a specimen that would leave a certified pimp speechless.

"Dee, this is Candy Red." Kiara handed me the suitcase and snapped me out of my trance.

"Candy, this the nigga you been waiting your whole life to meet." She led her by the hand until she was standing in front of me. My sister wasn't no slouch either, standing at a respectable five feet, eight inches with her light honey complexion and enough body to make a gay man pause. I was standing in front of two of the most beautiful women I'd ever seen in my life, and I'd only been out of prison for five minutes! Whew, it was gonna be a long day.

"How are you doing, sweetheart?" I asked her, setting the suitcase down and reaching for her hand. The smile she graced me with was nothing short of amazing as she took the hand I offered and pulled me into a welcomed hug.

"It's nice to finally meet you, Devaughn. Or should I call you Dee?"

"Baby, you can call me anything you want, just as lon—"

"Oh nigga, please, you gonna fuck her. Damn!" Kiara laughed and pushed Candy back toward the open car door. All I could do was laugh.

"Come on, let's get the fuck out of here," I said, grabbing the suitcase and climbing in the backseat next to the still-smiling Candy.

"Oh, so I'm your driver now, nigga? Boy, you better be lucky I love your big-head ass or you'd be walking!"

"Yeah, yeah, just drive this big muthafucka before they change their mind and I wake up back in my bunk."

"Car start. Autopilot, navigate to the nearest bank from this location," Kiara said before turning around to face us.

"Ayo, this ride can do all that?" I asked in complete amazement.

"Yeah, nigga, it'd be a piece of shit if it couldn't. But that ain't the best part, this muthafucka tricked out on some 007 type shit. I'm talking fully bulletproof and everything. If a muthafucka get me in this car, then he had something nuclear." She diligently cracked a blunt while the car drove itself.

"So, cars drive theyself, but you still gotta roll your own blunt? Ain't that a bitch." I opened the suitcase to inspect its contents.

"Nah, I ain't gotta roll it. I want to. Besides, when you hit this fire-ass black diamond, you will appreciate me keeping it old school."

"Whatever," was my response as I pulled out some all-black Gucci jeans, a white Gucci t-shirt and some black and white Gucci high-tops to match. "What's this, Kiara? I told you to bring me some sweats."

"Alright, first, stop using my birth name, because you named me Keyz, and that's what I go by. Secondly, this is 2022 and that sweatpants shit is played out. Besides, nigga, I can afford to buy Gucci if I wanted to, so relax." She put the finishing touches on the blunt, but didn't light it. I didn't feel like arguing, plus it was her show.

"Just chill, Papi," Candy rasped into my ear while kissing a fiery trail down my neck. All thoughts of clothes were forgotten as her lips and tongue danced across my skin in such an incredibly sensual way that I had to remind myself to breathe. Dropping the clothes to capture her dreads, I brought her mouth to mine, where I experienced a kiss so powerful I was sure I heard electricity humming. Her tongue tasted of ripe kiwi and strawberries, and her lips held the soft moisture of plums. I could feel myself getting lost in her aura, in her essence, and I was helpless to stop it as I let my hands roam the exquisite landscape of her figure.

"Well damn, that kiss was so serious it got me hot!" Her voice broke me out of my trance, made me pull back and gaze deeply into the eyes of this remarkable young woman.

"It'll be magic," I whispered against her lips, letting her go and picking my clothes back up. The smile on Keyz' face said it all — I still had it. I could hear Candy's heavy breathing, and I could only imagine how wet her pussy was at that exact moment. This thought brought a smile to my face while I prepared to change out of the depressing khaki uniform the state of Virginia had issued me to come home in.

"Wait a minute, bro, you can do that while I run into the bank real quick. I need the suitcase, though, so dump the rest of that shit on the backseat."

The rest of that shit was a small arsenal of guns that I'd suggested she pick up for me. A quick inventory revealed a .45 with a 21-shot clip full of black talons, an HKmp5 submachine gun with two 60-round clips, a baby Uzi with two 60 clips, and a four-barrel glock with two 32-round clips. All in all, it wasn't a bad start.

"Good job." I handed the bag over the seat. Her response was to blow me a kiss on her way out of the car. I quickly stripped the loathsome khakis off me and started to dress in my new clothes.

"You know, we've probably got at least fifteen minutes before Keyz comes back," Candy said, licking those soft, red lips seductively.

"It shouldn't take her that long," I replied, sliding my t-shirt over my head.

"Trust me." She took the jeans from my hands and pushing a button to slide the partition up between the front and back seats, closing us off from the world. The car was spacious, sort of like a miniature Maybach, but I was still worried about time constraints.

"Maybe we shou—"

"Shhh, un-uh, just let me handle this." She made quick work of her clothes until she was completely and beautifully naked in front of me. Speech and thought took leaps out the window as I pulled her into my lap and locked onto the mouth I was beginning to crave more and more. Our kisses alternated between soft and sweet to a frenzy that displayed our wants and needs loud and clear. Without breaking contact, she slid around until she was straddling my pulsing manhood that was aching to spear her to any seat available.

"Candy, I don't have a – *oh shit!*" was all I could say to the feeling of her taking me inside of her juicy, warm pussy in one downward stroke. Her moans were instantaneous as she began a slow gallop that forced all the air from my lungs. I could hear the wetness of her delicious pussy with every motion, and the sweet smell of it was enough to make my mouth water. Gripping her waist directly opposite of the tiger claws, I guided her up and down faster and faster, feeling her stretch and mold herself to me until two became one. I felt my climax coming, and the speed of it frightened me.

"Wait. Candy, I'm about to— To—"

"Me too," she replied, retaking control of the situation by spinning around until she was throwing pussy and perfectly-shaped ass back at me in abundance. Silence was not an option as I roared like the lion I was, and we both found the promise land of blissful climaxes. I couldn't move, could barely breathe, and couldn't believe the still-shaking woman I was buried inside of had worked me so thoroughly.

"I demand a run back," I said, laughing and caressing one half of her fat ass.

"You're telling me. I've never came that fast for anyone," she replied, getting off my lap and sliding onto the seat next to me.

"How old are you, Candy?"

"I'm 26, why?"

"And you mean to tell me that some lil' young nigga ain't digging up in you every chance he can get?" This earned me a laugh and a twinkle of mischief from her mesmerizing eyes.

"I don't really fuck with dudes. It's mainly me and Keyz. Don't get me wrong, the sex is mind-blowing, but I always take a while to cum. Which means, Mr. Mitchell, that you and I are gonna keep doing this until we figure out the winning formula. If that's alright with you." She dipped her head and took me in her mouth without hesitation. Words weren't possible. All I could do was run my fingers through her hair while she took what she so obviously wanted.

"Mmmm, damn girl, save some for later."

"But I'm hungry, Daddy," she purred, going right back to her feast. The sound of the car door opening brought me back from the edge as Keyz hopped back behind the wheel.

"Y'all ain't done yet?" she asked with mock irritation. As much as I didn't want to, I had to tell Candy to stop so I could put the rest of my clothes on. Surprisingly, she didn't follow my lead.

"Get dressed," I told her, kissing her one more time.

"For what?" she replied, again pushing the button and letting down the partition separating us from the front.

"That's what I'm talking about," Keyz said, climbing into the back of the car and sitting next to Candy.

"Okay, so who's gonna drive this muthafucka?" I asked, taking the blunt and lighter she was passing me.

"Well, first we need to know where you want to go before anything," she said, tracing lazy circles around Candy's nipples with her fingernail. I hadn't thought about where to go first. I hadn't even decided if I would get straight to business or allow myself some down time before shit kicked off.

"Who knows I'm out?" I asked, lighting the blunt and inhaling deeply.

"Nobody for real. I've been doing like you said and telling anyone who'll listen that you set your time back again. You already know that the only people who check the Department of Correction's website is Dog and your uncle." Dog was my brother, and I trusted him, so him knowing I was out wouldn't be a problem. My uncle was a totally different story, but I'd deal with him when the time was right.

"How many soldiers do we have?" I asked, hitting and passing the blunt.

"I did a roll call this morning, and we've got 150 in the metropolitan area, 300 in Tidewater, Virginia, about 100 in Durham, North Carolina, and 70 in different parts of Texas."

"I see you've spread out quite nicely." I rubbed my chin and did the numbers in my head.

"If it ain't broke, don't fix it. It's EMU, bitch," she replied around a mouthful of smoke directed at Candy. EMU was our set. The movement had grown a lot in the last 10 years, but it was good because my team was on some real get-money shit. We weren't a bunch of broke-ass gangbangers like society had been trying to label us since the 60s. We'd moved past that into the business of being entrepreneurs like our founding fathers had originally envisioned, and I was proud of my contribution to that. Like my man Knuckles once told me, every day I made history.

"Do you know where Mikko is?" I asked, a bitter taste flooding my mouth at the sound of her name.

"Yeah, but— Are you sure you wanna start there? I mean, that's kinda obvious," Keyz replied, passing me the blunt back and running her hands up and down Candy's body in a slow, sensual way.

"I'm just trying to see my kids before life gets hectic. I owe them that, at least." I could feel the effects of the weed when I felt the anxiety and tension leap off me in waves, pushing me deeper into the comfortable leather seats. I knew I had to think things through, because everything begins and ends with the mental, and any miscalculation was a one-way trip to the grave. Like I said, prison was off the menu.

"Alright." Keyz reluctantly climbed back into the front seat and tossed the suitcase over. "Hey, Dee, tighten Candy up for me. She's looking a little horny back there." Candy took that as her cue and sent the partition back up.

"You ever made love on a million dollars?" she asked, opening the suitcase and dumping piles of money on the floor.

Chapter 2

Remember Me?

I watched the scenery change with unseeing eyes, allowing my mind to see the cities and towns we passed through like they were, once upon a time. Nothing was the same anymore, mainly because everything seemed to be made of steel, glass, and solar paneling. Don't get me wrong, it wasn't a bad thing that the world existed almost solely on natural resources and energy, but these were strange times in strange places for me. Two decades had changed a lot, and for the first time I felt every bit of my thirty-eight years. Candy's sleeping form stirred gently in my lap, causing me to look at her with a smile on my face. Our second encounter had been everything I promised her, and I showed her why sometimes age made all the difference in the world. Keyz had to turn the still-pumping classic Jay-Z up to deafening levels to drown out her girl's screams of pleasure and pain that hurt so good. I'd even caught her lowering the partition just enough to catch a glimpse of the rigorous workout I was putting Candy through. I guess it was too much for her, because it didn't take her long to shut it again. Looking back out the window, I saw the city of Centreville for the first time like it is now, and I wondered if my kids would be happy to see me. This day of freedom was long since talked about, but even though it was here, it still couldn't take away the years of pain I'd caused them. Nothing could.

"We've got a problem, Dee," Keyz said, accelerating fast around a corner and cutting the music off.

"What is it?" I asked, shaking Candy lightly and handing her clothes to her.

"There's an all-black Monte Carlo behind us, and it's been there since the bank."

"Cops?"

"No, I don't think it's the people because I haven't exactly been maintaining the speed limit, so they could've pulled us."

"What's the plan?" I asked, grabbing the HKmp5 and slamming a clip in it, setting it on full automatic.

"The plan is that I'm gonna drive us into this dead end around the corner and stop. After that, you know what it is."

By now Candy was dressed and loading the baby Uzi with a childlike grin on her face. Keyz turned the car around in the dead end and brought us to a stop facing the way we'd entered. I took a cigarette from the pack in Candy's hand, lit it, and watched as the Monte Carlo bent the corner hesitantly. Obviously not one to play waiting games, Candy opened her door, concealing her weapon, and waved the now-idling car forward. I admired her spunk, but her challenge didn't have the desired affect, because whoever it was just sat there.

"Back in the car, Candy," I said, opening my door and stepping out into the bright morning sun. I stood there with the door hiding my gun, smoking a cigarette as if I didn't have a care in the world, staring intently at the two figures in the car. Slowly, their car started to move forward, almost like it was being pulled by an unseen puppet master. I took a quick look around to see if any unsuspecting witnesses lurked about. Satisfied that I was reasonably safe, I took one last pull on my smoke and passed it to Keyz.

"Hold that, Light Skin, while I go talk to these nice gentlemen."

Chambering the first round into the gun, I stepped from behind the car door and opened fire. Bullets flew, glass shattered, and I heard the vague sounds of screams as I emptied the clip into the fast-fleeing car. I couldn't help but laugh, watching the driver sideswipe two cars and a mailbox trying to get away as fast as possible, knowing that whomever it was made a serious miscalculation that I'd be unarmed or timid. Climbing back into the car, I took the still-smoldering cigarette Keyz handed me and sat back while she smoothly guided us back to the main road.

"Who do you think it was, Dee?" Keyz asked, picking up her cellphone.

"If I had to guess, I'd say it was probably Rebekah and Renee's stupid-ass brothers, but I'm sure we'll know soon enough. Did you get the plates?"

"Yep, that's what I'm running right now. Why you so quiet Candy?" I asked, putting out the cigarette and turning to face her.

"I'm good," she replied, still holding onto the baby Uzi.

"I know you good, boo, but you're just quiet. I hope I didn't scare you," I took the gun from her hands and placed her hands in mine. I was searching her face intently for any sign that she couldn't be trusted, because loyalty was the name of the game we played, and anything that didn't fit the mold would be eliminated without questions.

"Scare me?" she laughed, scooting closer to me again. "Actually, you turned me on," she whispered, kissing me slowly and softly on the lips. She didn't know that I'd mastered my desires, especially those of the flesh, so I wouldn't allow myself to be controlled by lust. Her words sounded genuine, but I'd still keep my eyes on her and find out everything I could from Keyz before I made a decision on her fate.

"Last name Taylor." Keyz lowered the phone and looked at me with a question in her eyes.

"No, take me to Mikko's house."

She said something else into the phone before hanging up and driving on in deep thought.

"What is it, K?"

"I just think that we should eliminate them today. I can have it done while you're meeting with your PO later."

Damn, if the whole Taylor family disappeared on my first day home, I was guaranteed to cast the most suspicion. They might even take me in for questioning. Monica Taylor was the reason I'd gone to prison in the first place, because as they say, "Hell hath no fury like a woman scorned." She and I were never a couple — more like friends with benefits. Then one day she drops a bomb on me and tells me she is pregnant. The baby wasn't the problem. The fact that she wanted me to leave my wife and other two kids, well, that was just plain unacceptable. Even as a young man, I was man enough to take care of my responsibilities, and I told her that our child would want for nothing, but somehow that wasn't enough. So when her demands of $10,000 were met with a not-so-subtle laugh and a fuck you, I found myself in handcuffs, facing a crime fit for the mind of a sexual deviant. All it took were three lying-ass little words from her juvenile sisters — "He touched me." — and my life as I knew it was over. My mind was made up then that they would pay, all of them, right down to the baby she claimed was mine.

"Do it," I replied harshly, contemplating the results of the actions in connection with the rest of my plans. I wanted to rush what had to be done because I fully intended to enjoy a lot of it, but plans were made to be followed, and I knew how things had to go.

"What's on your mind, Dee?" Candy asked, rolling another blunt with the speed and expertise of a veteran smoker.

"I got a lot on my mind, Red, and a lot of loose ends to tie up before the day is over."

"Don't even sweat all that, Papi, you know we got you."

"Is that right?" I asked, looking at her for the first time and wondering what was under the hood.

"Of course that's right. You lead, we follow until you tell or show us that it's our time to lead. You're Caesar and we're Rome, the new Rome, so just have patience and trust us, okay?"

Her statements set me back just a little, made me think of what could be lost or gained by trying to carry too much of the burden myself. I had to admit that she made sense, and I liked that.

"Baby, most people don't know it, but Caesar was quite gay. But I understand what you're saying and why you're saying it. Know this, though: be careful of how much intelligence you display, because it increases the levels of accountability dramatically. A wise man can play a fool, but a fool can't play a wise man."

"Very true, but see, I play my position, and my position for you is any and everything you need it to be. However, that only works if you know I'm capable," she replied, lighting the sweet-smelling ganja and inhaling mightily.

"Touché."

"Dee, we're here, and that looks like Latavia right there in the doorway." At the mention of my oldest daughter's name, I flung the car door open and stepped from the ride slowly so as to fully observe my surroundings. All I could do was stare in amazement at the beautiful young woman with her back toward me, thinking back to when she was just a little girl who hated to eat any type of vegetables. She was my secret Daddy's girl, the one who didn't really show it in front of me but was downright possessive when it came down to it. I laughed as I thought about the time she dragged a poor little girl by her hair because she felt I was giving the girl too much attention. That was my baby, the sneaky passive-aggressive one.

"I'll be back in time for dinner, Mom!" she yelled into the house, closing the door and immediately seeing me standing by the car. "Holy shit," she murmured, leaning against the door with her hand to her chest. She looked just like her mother did at that age, only slimmer and, from what I could tell, a lot fewer tattoos. At twenty-two, she was beautiful with eyes the color of warm chocolate and skin that looked like heated rosewood in the summer's morning light. The only thing missing was that megawatt smile that I knew she still had.

"Don't look so happy to see me." I walked up the steps and stopping right in front of her.

"It's— it's not that. I just can't believe you're out. I didn't think you were ever coming home," she whispered, trying to keep the tears in her eyes from falling. I didn't know what to say. How could I begin to explain the sacrifice I'd made for her, her sisters, and her mother all those years ago? Truthfully, I should've come home sixteen years ago, but when my wife got caught on a phone tap ordering the deaths of Monica's family, I did what I had to do. I couldn't let my six-month-pregnant wife go to prison, and so I did what was the unthinkable for my whole family: I took the charge. Now, standing in front of my oldest joy in the world, I knew that secret was better left buried.

"I told you they couldn't hold me forever. Can I get a hug?" I asked, extending my arms. And then the tears did fall as she stepped into my embrace, hugging me tightly to make sure I was real and not a figment of her imagination. I hugged her back as strong as I dared, not wanting to hurt her, yet not wanting to let her go either. "I missed you so much, baby girl," I told her, tears rolling soundlessly down my face.

"Me too, Daddy, I missed you, too."

It was time I faced the rest of my diva squad, as they were known.

"Come on, come back into the house for a little while." When I tried to steer us toward the front door, I met immediate resistance.

"Um. Dad, that's not really a good idea right now." I saw a touch of panic swim through her eyes, and I knew the reason for it.

"Trust me, sweetheart, I'm not looking for trouble." I signaled Keyz and Candy to join me. I could tell by the windbreaker that Keyz had slipped on that she was holding, and Candy still had her hands behind her back in her best innocent girl pose.

"Hey, Latavia, what's up?" Keyz stepped forward to give her a hug while Candy passed me the .45 that I tucked in the back of my jeans.

"'Sup, Kiara," she replied, sizing up Candy the whole time. "And you are?" she asked, stepping around Keyz until she was face to face with who she obviously felt was someone who didn't belong.

"I'm Keyz's girlfriend, Candy." She answered both the spoken and unspoken questions without hesitation or fear.

"La-La, come on." I pulled her by her arm so she could open the front door. It was no longer my right to walk into my baby's mama's house, and I respected that because no more fuel needed to be added to the inferno that we were.

"Are you sure, Dad?" she asked with her hand on the doorknob.

"Yeah, baby, I'm sure."

"Well, here goes nothing. *Mom!*" she yelled, opening the door and leading us into the house.

"What, Latavia?" Mikko yelled back, obviously agitated by something or someone.

"Dad's here."

"What the fuck is Damanya doing here?" she asked. I could hear her moving upstairs, coming toward us, but the staircase faced the back of the house.

"I said my Dad, not my sperm donor," Latavia replied testily.

"Devaughn?" Mikko rounding the corner suddenly. She was just like I'd remembered. Too vain to be taken hostage by gray hair without a fight, I admired her golden dreadlocks that just touched her shoulders. Her skin was still that dazzling light brown that reminded me of a sunset in some far-off land. The succulent mouth that stood agape was even more tantalizing now with the slight lines of age surrounding it than it had been all those years ago.

Aryanna

After having five kids, she'd aged well and even slimmed down a little. But looks hadn't been her problem — fidelity had.

"Hello, Mikko." I stepped further into the house, allowing everyone in behind me so we could close the door.

"How— When— How did you get out?" she asked, flopping into the nearest seat, which happened to be in the living room.

"My time was up, or did you forget my max-out date?"

"I know, but you told me that you'd gotten more time for something."

"I just wanted to surprise everyone. Surprise." I moved past Latavia and taking a seat across from Mikko. She honestly looked like a beautiful deer caught in headlights, but I knew it wasn't shock as much as it was fear that had her looking at me so weirdly.

"Shit. I need a cigarette." She patted her empty pockets. I nodded toward Candy, who gave her a light before stepping over to stand beside my chair.

"And who are you?" Mikko asked in that polite nastiness that was her trademark. It was as if she'd just noticed there were other people in the room besides us.

"She's not your concern," I replied, taking the lit cigarette Candy offered me and pulling her into the seat next to me.

"Dad," Latavia growled at me with a look that said *be nice*. Mikko seemed to regain some of her composure, because she sat back on the couch and studied me with a fire in her eyes that I'd seen before. It was the fire of possession.

"Where's Day-Day and Deshana?" I asked, referring to my other two daughters Mikko and I shared. Sharday was twenty years old, and out of all of my girls, she was the biggest daddy's girl. I went in when she was only 13 months old, but the bond we had only grew stronger with time. Now Deshana, on the other hand, was my 18-year-old twin. She looked like me, acted like me, and much to the annoyance of her mother, she was just as smart as I was. All my children were intelligent. Latavia went to

Georgetown, where she majored in criminal justice and was taking classes to become a lawyer. Day-Day was enrolled at Howard University, where she was the star of their music program. And now that Deshana had graduated, it was up to her where she went to school. All in all, I was very proud of my diva squad, because while they were all like me in some way, they'd succeeded this far without me.

"Well, let's see. Day-Day and Deshana are upstairs sleeping. And Jordyn — you remember her, right? — well, she's upstairs with her daddy." One look at Latavia and I could see the fear was back, as well as a silent plea for me not to lose my composure. I could tell Mikko was hoping to throw me off balance as I'd done her by bringing up the first child she had with another nigga while I was gone. Add to that that the nigga in question was upstairs sleeping like a baby and we were walking through Hell with gasoline drawers on. I caught Keyz giving me the *I wouldn't kill the nigga here unless he provoked me to* look

"And your son, how is he?" I replied casually, still smoking my cigarette. The fact I wasn't ruffled seemed to bother her even more, because the word *fine* came out in a deep growl as she puffed away on her cigarette. I couldn't help but smile. "La-La, will you go wake your sisters up so I can take you all to breakfast?"

Without a word, she got up and started toward the stairs.

"Oh, don't forget Jordyn," I said, never taking my gaze from the now bug-eyed face of my ex-wife.

"Daddy," Latavia said again in that voice that told me I was pushing again.

"It's only fair, Latavia, now go ahead," I replied, putting my cigarette out. "Would you like to join us, Mikko?" I asked, all innocence and charm.

"It seems you have quite enough company as it is. Besides, I don't want you to spend your whole little $25 check in one spot," she replied, smirking.

"That reminds me. Candy, run out to the car and bring me ten apiece for the kids, all five of them." I smacked her ass for good measure and caught the mischief dancing in Keyz's eyes.

"Ten? Wow, big spender," Mikko kicked her feet up on the chipped wooden coffee table. I didn't respond. Instead I looked around at what could have been a nice house if the right decorations were applied. The living room was spacious with wall-to-wall carpeting, but the oversized couch and entertainment center made it look like a cluttered mess. It was clean, though, which I guess was all that mattered when you were on a fixed income. Maybe she'd be able to do more once I moved the girls into their own spot.

"Daddy!" screamed my two girls in unison as they came flying down the stairs and hopped into my lap.

"Damn, y'all got huge on me," I replied, hugging them tightly. My little girls had grown into not-so-little women and filled out enough to make me glad I was carrying a big gun.

"When did you get home, Dad?" Day-Day asked.

"About two hours ago, actually. Come on, you should've already knew where my first stop was going to be," I replied, looking back and forth between my two beautiful women.

"We thought you still had more time to do," Deshana whispered, tears clouding her eyes and spilling over onto her face.

"Come on, baby, don't cry. I'm home now, and I'm not going anywhere."

"Oh, you're going somewhere, nigga, because you ain't staying here," Craig said, coming down the stairs wearing sweatpants, some boots, and a grin on his face. It was at this moment that Candy came back in with the money I'd sent her to get, and the look on her face told me the tension in the air was evident.

"Are you even allowed to be here, nigga?" Craig asked, sitting next to Mikko and putting a possessive arm around her.

"Daddy, don't," Latavia said, obviously seeing the anger and hatred flash in my eyes. Mikko saw it, too, because she put her hand on his knee and whispered something to him.

"You girls go get dressed so I can take you out to eat," I said softly, pushing them from my lap.

"Who said they was going with you?" he asked like he had all the rights in the world to say anything to me about my children. Nobody moved. It seemed like no one was breathing.

"Craig, this ain't what you want," I replied calmly.

"Girls, you heard your father, now get dressed." Keyz led them quickly from the room.

"What, am I supposed to be scared of you because you was in the pen, muthafucka? You was in there for some pussy shit, for touchin' on—"

He never finished his sentence before I was out of my seat with my .45 smiling sweetly in his face.

"Go ahead, say it, you bitch-ass nigga, and you'll die right here, now. Go ahead, I bet you won't say it. Matter fact, open your mouth, bitch." I cocked the hammer on the pistol and shoved it savagely between his teeth. "These are the crimes I got away with, nigga! I murdered pussies like you in these streets, so you best remember that and me, because the next time I see you, it's the last time I see you." I was so mad I was shaking, and I could hear the gun barrel rattling around against his teeth. I wanted to kill him, I wanted to blow a nice hole through his head. And I probably would've if I didn't see her standing there with her big doe eyes looking at me, almost through me.

"Please don't shoot my daddy," Jordyn whispered. I had every right to kill him, but I wouldn't do it in front of his little girl. Maybe someday a nigga would grant me that courtesy.

"Mikko, I suggest that you tell your boyfriend, fiancé, or whatever the fuck he is that I'm not the one." I looked at her squarely before taking the gun out of his mouth. I could tell two things when I looked at her: one, she was scared for her own life, and two, it turned her on in a way that nothing had in twenty years. She'd done things, horrible things, in order to forget the love she had for me and hopefully the reason why she loved me. As she licked her lips and slowly shook her head, I could tell she hadn't forgotten shit. She remembered exactly what it was.

Chapter 3

Am I a Monster?

The car was full, but the conversation was strained. Nobody really wanted to comment on what happened back there, but at the same time, no one except Jordyn knew what really happened. The inevitable question came.

"Daddy, what did you do when we went upstairs?" Latavia asked quietly. I'd been gone a long time, and that's why Day-Day and Deshana only had stories of me for most of their memories, but Latavia was old enough to remember my anger and how nothing good ever came from that.

"Does it matter?" I asked, looking out the window at the cars on the highway.

"Dad, don't be like that, because you've always promised us honesty."

I knew she was right, just like I knew I'd have to tell them the truth when they came back downstairs and saw Jordyn holding onto her father like he might disappear any moment. I was mad at myself for losing my temper like that, but I couldn't take it back now.

"You girls aren't babies anymore, so I'm not gonna treat you like you are. What I will tell you is don't ever ask me a question that you don't want the answer to. I've tried to keep you ignorant of me and the things I'm capable of, but if you insist on asking me, I'm not gonna lie about it. So, I ask you: do you want an answer to that question, Latavia?" I looked directly at her for the first time since we'd gotten in the car. I could see the uncertainty in her eyes, but she was my daughter, and I knew she wouldn't back down.

"Yes," she replied in a strong and clear voice.

"Keyz, where are we going to eat?" I asked.

"We're going to Old Country Buffet in Manassas, and we'll be there in about ten minutes." I didn't know exactly what I planned to say, but I figured ten minutes would cover it.

"Candy, pass me the suitcase back here. I'ma show you girls what my life really consists of so there won't be any questions about your father as a man," I told them, opening the suitcase so they could see the money and guns. Then I took the .45 from out of the back of my jeans and sat it on my lap. "I put this gun in Craig's mouth with the intention of blowing his muthafuckin' head off for disrespecting me, but Jordyn asked me not to shoot her dad, and I didn't. In my world, disrespect is not tolerated, but I tried to let it go on the strength of your mother, mainly. Dude somehow felt that I was some type of bitch, and I reacted accordingly. I'm a member of one of the most ruthless criminal organizations that've ever existed in the known world, and I take that very seriously, but what you see before you is only a small part of everything. I've been out of prison for three hours, and I'm riding around in a million-dollar car with a million in a suitcase and a few toys to keep me company. So, to sum this little speech up, I'm your father, and I love you more than life, but I'm also a gangsta with a lot of responsibilities." I was honest and to the point, and they would either love me or hate me for it.

"Have you killed someone before?" Deshana asked in a surprisingly calm voice. At first all I did was look at her, trying to gauge whether or not she could handle the truth.

"Yeah," I replied simply, choosing not to elaborate because now was not the time for glorifying or trading war stories.

"Dad, we've always known that you loved us and you wouldn't do anything to hurt us, so my question is are we in danger because of the life you lead?" Day-Day asked, looking back and forth between me and the suitcase.

"No," Keyz said from the front seat. "So far your father's activities have been restricted to the inside for obvious reasons, and the only one operating on his orders in these streets is me. I've been careful in making sure that our life hasn't spilt over into yours, which is why I don't get to see you as often as I'd like."

"You're part of this too, Kiara?" Latavia said with obvious disgust.

"Yeah," she replied, looking directly at Latavia in the rearview mirror.

"So what the fuck are we supposed to be, some type of criminal family now? The only reason I went to school to become a fucking lawyer is because you were taken away from us for some complete bullshit, but now I see that I'm probably still gonna end up defending your ass in court anyway!"

No one said a word. Everyone just waited to see what my reaction was gonna be to her rants and accusations.

"I am what I am, Latavia, and I've never claimed to be perfect. The only thing I've ever claimed to do is love you unconditionally. Can you do the same?"

Everyone was looking at her, waiting and wondering what, if anything, could be agreed to as we pulled into the parking lot of the restaurant. I'd taken off my mask and revealed the boogieman underneath, but I didn't know if that was the right decision now. I saw the pain in my daughters' faces, the uncertainty of what I was really capable of and if the sins of the parent would someday be visited on them. A promise that would never happen would seem hollow to my ears, so all I could do was wait.

"I love you, Dad — unconditionally. Just promise that you'll do your best to protect the family and yourself now that you're home." She curled up on my lap like she use to when she was little.

"I promise you that, and I also promise that no matter what happens, I'ma keep on loving you. Now, I'm starving, so can we eat, please?" I asked, opening the door and closing the suitcase before getting out of the car.

We all piled out of the car and stormed the restaurant like a group that hadn't eaten in years. We spent the next two hours laughing, joking, and enjoying both the food as well as the company, and for once forgetting the pain of the past. I knew it was the little moments like this in life that I'd have to hold on to when the coldness of my life became too much for me to bear. I'd never been one to seek happiness because I'm a firm believer that contentment works just fine, or satisfaction as the least, but right there I was actually happy for the first time in a long time. In the back of my mind, I still knew a lot of people had to die, but even that didn't sadden me.

"Candy, you still got that?" I asked, referring to the money from earlier. She passed me three stacks under the table with a wink and a smile in my direction. "Alright, ladies, so this is what it is. I'm home now, and the means that you all no longer have to worry about anything." I handed them each a stack of money. "That don't mean that you're not gonna finish school or that you won't start school, Deshana. What this means is that I'm gonna help you in any way that I can, and for starters, I think it's time you all got your own place."

"Now, Dad, when you say our own place, do you mean individually or one house together?" Day-Day asked, doing a quick count of the $10,000 in her hand.

"Separate, fully-furnished apartments until you finish school, and then we'll go from there. But if you think niggas gonna be running in and out, you got the game fucked up, and I hope you know that."

"What if I said I wanted to be a part of the movement?" Deshana asked quietly, causing the whole table to go silent.

"Excuse me?" I replied, not sure I heard her right.

"What if I said that I was ready and willing to be a part of your world, Dad?"

"What makes you think you're built for that?" I asked, slowly sipping my orange juice.

"I'll show you." She leaned over and whispered something to Candy. I couldn't hear what they were heatedly discussing, but the look Candy gave me said there was an obvious problem.

"Keyz, you, Day-Day, and Latavia go to the car now," Candy said without taking her eyes off of me.

"But—"

"Don't. Just go, Latavia," I said, holding up my hand to silence whatever argument she was planning to give.

"Dee, go ahead and pay the bill and follow them to the car."

I scanned my surroundings, still not spotting whatever danger Deshana had obviously located with an untrained eye.

"I'm not going anywhere. Which one of ya'll got a gun?"

"Dad, we can handle this, and you don't need to be in here right now," she replied, flashing me my own four-barrel glock from the suitcase.

"Sneaky muthafucka." I got up and made my way to the counter.

When I got there, I finally saw them in the booth, sitting there like nothing was wrong. All I could do was shake my head and laugh, because I could only wonder what was going through Craig's mind as he sat there with his homeboys. One thing was for sure: he wouldn't be expecting whatever was coming next. Without looking back, I walked out of the restaurant and slid into the backseat of the waiting car. As soon as I got in, three pairs of eyes drilled me with expectant looks, and I noticed that Keyz was now holding the baby Uzi like a life preserver.

"What's going on, Dad?" Latavia asked first.

"I don't know, but I'm confident that your sister can take care of herself."

No sooner had I uttered the words than I heard Candy's voice saying "Pop the trunk." The car sunk down on its springs a little as we took on more weight. I knew that feeling — there were definitely at least two bodies in the trunk. I hid my grin behind the blunt that I was struggling to light while Candy and Deshana hopped in the car without a word.

"Let's go," I said to Keyz, inhaling heavily on the weed and holding the smoke until it felt as if my lungs would collapse.

"So, are we supposed to act like nothing happened?" Latavia asked with obvious and blatant annoyance.

"Yeah." Deshana took the blunt from my hand and hit it twice before passing it to Candy so she could blow her a shotgun.

"Witnesses?" I asked reluctantly.

"None," Deshana said, choking on all the smoke in her lungs and coughing mightily.

"That ain't no dirt weed, slim," Keyz said, signaling for the blunt next.

"How many?" I asked.

"All of them," Candy replied, lighting a cigarette and passing it to me. These two pint-sized women had abducted three niggas in broad daylight without there being one witness to the crime, and that was quite a job. On top of that, they were as cool as the other side of the pillow.

"You know that still don't prove shit, right?" I asked Deshana, passing her the cigarette. Her smile caused me to shiver a little bit. For a split second, she looked exactly like me twenty years ago.

"What the fuck you mean *what happens next*, Deshana? What happens next is that our dear old dad is gonna take us the fuck home before we inadvertently get caught up in some shit. Ain't that right, Dad?" she asked, fixing me with a stare that said *remember your promise to keep us safe*. I knew she was right, and I wasn't about to argue with her all day.

"Keyz, how much time before the PO thing?"

"We've got about five hours before her office closes, but we could always show up at her house," she replied, smiling and passing the blunt back over the seat.

"Nah, too early for house calls. Let's drop Latavia and Day-Day off at the house real quick."

"What about Deshana?" Latavia asked.

"Deshana, how old are you?" I asked, passing her the blunt and taking my cigarette back.

"Dad, you know I'm 18. My birthday is tattooed on your hand."

"Yeah, I know how old you are, but for some reason your sister has forgotten that you're grown, so I was asking for her benefit."

"Deshana, you can't be serious. You're just— you're just gonna go with him?"

"Latavia, this *him* is our father, and you muthafuckin' right I'm going with him. Look, sis, I love you, and you know that, so just trust me. Dad ain't gonna do shit to hurt me, and deep down you know that, too."

It seemed as if we were at a crossroads again, but I knew this time it was between them and not me. My children had grown up and developed minds and opinions of their own, and as their father, it was my duty to let them think for themselves.

"Dad?" Latavia said, looking at me with her heart in her eyes.

"What is it that you want me to say, La-La? I've never forced right or wrong on you, only the reality that you will have to live and suffer with the consequences of both. Would you prefer I was a hypocrite and said that it was okay for me and your aunt to be Bloods, but none of you can? Do you remember when you were little and didn't want to eat your vegetables? What did I use to tell your mom?"

"That you didn't eat them, so we didn't have to either," she replied with a reluctant smile.

"Do as I say, not as I do has never been real good in my parenting book, unless the situation was extreme. And before you say anything, know and understand that I ain't never killed a nigga who didn't deserve to die."

"La-La, I just want to spend some time with Dad, okay? Don't trip. I'm still gonna be the same loveable me in the morning who listens to you and your boyfriend make kissy faces over the phone." She laughed at Latavia's sudden blush as she looked directly at me.

"Trust me." I pushed a piece of hair that escaped from her ponytail back behind her ear as the car came to a stop in front of their house. "You okay, Day-Day?" I asked, turning to face my one child who'd been silent for the whole ride.

"I'm fine, Daddy, I'm just glad you're home." She slid over to give me a hug and a kiss.

"Give your mom this money and tell her to call Keyz if she needs anything," I said, opening the door and stepping out of the car. I could hear our guests getting restless in the trunk. "Keyz, turn the music up. Listen, girls, if anyone asks where you got money from, tell them you got it from your aunt. It's still a secret that I'm home, so don't tell nobody until I let you know."

"Alright, Dad, I love you," Day-Day said, giving me another hug and walking toward the house.

"I love you too, baby. Come on, La-La, give me a hug. You know you want to." I wrapped my arms around her.

"Daddy, just be careful, please," she murmured against my chest, holding onto me like I might blow away in the breeze.

"I got you, babe," I said, kissing the top of her head and watching her go in the house as I climbed back in the ride.

"Alright, now what?" I asked my entourage of three.

"Well, apparently this is now Deshana's show, because she's informed me of what she needs and why she needs it," Keyz said, pushing the car at a fast clip.

"So, what's the deal, Lil' Me?" I'd been calling her Little Me since she was born, and as it turned out, I might've been more right than I knew.

"We're going out to Keyz's spot so I can have a nice chat with these gentlemen, and when that conversation is concluded, I guess you and I will have a talk too, Dad."

Candy was silent, but the words behind her eyes said enough.

"You agree, Candy?"

"I do. I think that since she spotted the threat, she should be the one to talk to our friends in the trunk first."

I guess I was out-voted, but this was an opportunity to find out how sound Candy's judgment was and what Deshana was made of. Her following in my footsteps wasn't an ideal plan, but I was a firm believer that my kids wouldn't learn how to do wrong the wrong way. I lost a lot of homies growing up because their parents chose to show willful ignorance and left it up to the streets to teach their children. In the end, those same parents were taught how unforgiving and merciless the streets could be, but the cost of that lesson was a high price to pay. Sitting back in my seat, I enjoyed the ride as we left the city and ventured into the country. The scenery was nice and relaxing, but I couldn't really enjoy it because Keyz was pushing the shit out of the car.

"Ayo, drive like you know it's three niggas in the trunk."

"Boy, please, I got this. I told you this muthafucka was tricked out. What, you think I ain't got radar?" she asked, pressing down harder on the gas pedal.

"Okay, Miss Radar, but if the peoples sneak up on us, then it ain't gonna matter, because I'm shootin'."

All she did was laugh at me while motioning for Candy to climb into the front seat with her.

"Before I forget, is everything set up for that other situation later on?"

"Yeah, all I've gotta do is make the call when you're at your PO's office, because the house is already under surveillance."

"I was thinking, it might be kinda risky snatching that many people, so we might need more than just a few guys for this."

"Already ahead of you. That's why we already had someone take the four main targets, since they lived together, and the rest will be picked up separately. Nobody disappears until you have that alibi, though."

"Do you think we could hold the main ones on ice? I kinda wanted to do them myself." I could tell by the disapproving look she was giving me that wasn't a good idea. At the same time, I knew she could respect how personal it was for me.

"Are you sure?"

"Yeah, I'm absolutely positive."

"Fine, I'll make it happen. I'll have them brought to the house now." She picked up her cellphone, still not changing the disapproving look on her face.

"Who are you talking about, Dad?"

"You'll see," I answered, smiling a smile of sweet satisfaction and long overdue justice. We made the rest of the trip in a comfortable silence, only slightly interrupted by the welcome sounds of the *Miseducation of Lauryn Hill* leaking through the speakers. My mind constantly jumped back and forth between past and present and occasionally went on into the future. For me, it wasn't so much about what the future held as it was to actually have a future. Twenty-five years ago, I would've bet everything I had and ever dreamed of having that I wouldn't see thirty-eight years old. Saying thirty-eight was like saying ninety or 100 back then, but I'd made it, and now I had my sights set further down the line.

"We're here," Keyz announced, climbing from the car and going to the trunk. Candy stood next to her with the baby Uzi, and Deshana took up the other side with the HKmp5. Since this wasn't my show, I just stepped back and watched my three beautiful and very dangerous ladies work their magic.

"Okay, you stupid muthafuckas, get the fuck out of my car!" Keyz yelled, sticking a pearl-handled 9mm berretta in Craig's eye socket. I could tell he wanted to say something, wanted to cuss and scream and make empty threats, but he hadn't figured out whether he'd live or die yet. He couldn't roll the dice all the time.

I left them to the work of herding the cattle, so to speak, and I turned around to admire Keyz's big-ass house. There was green grass as far as the eye could see and three different fountains spread around the driveway, spraying some of the bluest water imaginable. I couldn't see any other houses around us, just wide open land and something like a smaller version of the main house off in the distance. I didn't know what to say. My twenty-four-year-old little sister was living in a fucking mansion! A smile creased my face when I walked up the stairs and through the doors that seemed to open like magic from a movie set.

"Shit," I mumbled, walking into the foyer and immediately noticing the twin staircases that seemed like they were only one step below the clouds. The roof was made of glass allowing the sun to throw blazing rays off of the rose-colored marble floors that surrounded me. Looking up, I saw the biggest chandelier I'd ever seen, and with the sunlight moving through it, rainbows bounced everywhere. It was too much. This was the type of house seen on TV or in the magazines, but not in the life of a hustler — unless it was Frank Lucas.

"Welcome home, Mr. Mitchell," said a petite Spanish woman who materialized from nowhere.

"Thank you."

"My name is Tara, and I work for you and your sister. Would you like me to show you to your wing of the house?"

"My wing?" I asked slowly, still not believing that my baby sister was living like Bruce Wayne by day and Rayful Edmonds by night.

"Yes sir. If you'll just follow me to the elevator." She turned and walked underneath the staircase. The wall opened up and we stepped aboard the elevator for the brief ride to the top of the house. "You'll be staying in the north wing." She made a right out of the elevator and escorted me through a twenty-foot archway that boasted doors with EMU engraved into the wood. Behind the doors stood a spacious hallway with thick red carpet that looked like it easily stretched for a quarter of a mile.

"What's the layout of the house?" I asked, still following her lead.

"There are twelve bedrooms, six in each wing. Ten and a half baths, a swimming pool, library, movie theater, full gym equipped with weights and a regulation basketball court, a conference room that seats twenty, and an indoor sauna and Jacuzzi. Now, you probably noticed the miniature house down the way a little bit. Well, that's for parties and entertainment purposes, because Ms. Keyz don't like everybody up in her shit."

"Understandable. I notice that there's clothing in the other rooms we've passed. Who's staying there?" I asked, coming to a stop behind her at the door to the master suite. Tara graced me with a smile that went all the way to her beautiful gray eyes, but she said not one word and simply opened the double doors in front of us. An enormous king size bed sat front and center when we walked through the doors. The color scheme of the room was harmonious shades of black and red, matching and complementing the plush carpet beneath my feet. Two nightstands the size of coffee tables surrounded my bed, and the matching armoires were posted to my left next to the windows. I could see into my bathroom, where my Jacuzzi tub sat filled with bubbles and black rose petals, and suddenly the sounds of Jaheim escaped from somewhere hidden. To my immediate right was my walk-in closet filled to capacity with clothes and shoes from labels and designers I'd never heard of, but the quality of the product was evident.

I took all this in with one smooth swing of my head from left to right, but the sight of the things on my bed caused me to pause and rub my hands across my face to conceal my excitement. Before me were five young women in various shades, shapes, and ethnic backgrounds, but every one of them was breathtaking and almost completely naked.

"Close your mouth, nigga, damn." Keyz pushed me in my back and laughed.

"What is this, K? Don't get me wrong, because I'm down for whatever, but— Mmm, damn, am I ever gonna get some sleep?"

"Nigga, you told me that it didn't matter where we lived as long as we were together and I kept 'options' around the house. Meet options." She pushed me all the way into the room.

"Mmm, damn, you're a sexy muthafucka," said a four foot, nine inch dark chocolate angel, running her hands underneath my shirt and then pulling it over my head.

"You not too bad yourself, baby," I said huskily, taking her hand and watching intently as she did a slow twirl, showing off her firm, plump ass.

"Hold up, DC." Keyz stopped me from being led to the bed where the rest of the women patiently awaited my arrival.

"What?" I asked, throwing a confused look at my sister.

"We got bidness to handle, nigga. Come on, stay focused. DC and the rest will wait 'til later, won't you, ladies?"

"Yes, Daddy," they replied in the sexiest harmony since Destiny's Child.

"DC stands for Dangerously Chocolate," she said, licking lazy circles around both of my nipples and squeezing my crotch lightly.

"Oh shit. Come on, Keyz, because in a minute there ain't gonna be no turning back." I walked out of the room and back down the hallway in a daze.

"Damn, nigga, do you want your shirt?" she asked, walking behind me, laughing hard.

"Nah, I ain't trying to get blood on it, anyway," I replied, holding the elevator door.

"You ready?" she asked, pushing a button.

"I've got twenty years of pent-up rage to unleash. Ready? Trust me, you don't even know the half of it."

The doors opened onto a brightly-lit basketball court where a rigorous game of five-on-five was taking place.

"Everybody on the court has rank and position, but you'll meet them later." Keyz led me through a side door.

The room we walked into was cold, and not just temperature-wise. It was cold. I'm sure I didn't even want to know half the stories these walls could tell. The room was bare except for two sets of running lights overhear, a cooler with some tools leaning against it, and three bodies strapped to three chairs. Deshana stood next to the gagged men, pistol in hand, and a look of determined violence on her face. Walking toward her, I noticed the large drain directly under Craig's chair and the pleading look in his eyes.

"Don't look at me. I'm just a spectator in all this." I took the chair Keyz offered me.

"Being that I know you have a lot to do, Dad, I don't want to waste a lot of time," she said, chambering the first round into a chrome .44.

"Nice gun."

"Thanks. Now then, I don't know you two muthafuckas, so you're really of no importance to me. I just want you to know that this is all Craig's fault." With that, she stepped to the guy on her left and shot him twice in the face.

"It's okay, boo," she told the second man, who was screaming for all he was worth behind the gag in his mouth. "Look at me. It's okay, I promise," she said sweetly, placing the gun under his chin and squeezing the trigger. She killed with the clinical detachment of a professional, making me wonder if this was her first kill. I felt my pulse quicken while watched my daughter work, watched the same beast that lived in me come to life in her and, for a moment, I was actually disturbed.

"Keyz, I need that special brew." She stuck the gun in the back of her hip-hugging jeans and pulled the gag from Craig's mouth.

"Deshana, what the fuck is wrong with you?" he screamed with spit, tears, and snot racing down his face.

"My dear Craig," she said, punching him hard enough to draw blood from his mouth.

"I've done nothing but treat you right, Deshana. Please don't do this. Think of Jordyn."

"Jordyn, Jordyn. Did you ever think about me, Craig? Do you ever stop and consider how you treating me like I was worthless because my last name is Mitchell made me feel? You could never take that my mother loved my father more than any nigga she's ever been with! And you took that out on me, you sorry motherfucker. Guess what? It's my turn now. Hey, Dad, I got some old-school flavor for you." She walked behind Craig and snatched his head back. I saw the glitter of steel in her mouth, and I knew what was coming. "Smile forever, bitch!" She pulled the straight razor from her mouth and sliced him from mouth to ear on both sides of his face. That wasn't the worst part. When she let his hair go and slapped him on his cuts, his face opened up like a pussy, and while he screamed I could see his teeth through the side of his jaw. I thought now would probably be the time she put a bullet in his head, but when Keyz came back carrying a pot that was still boiling, I knew the situation was serious.

"Deshana."

"I got this, Dad." She took the pot and gloves and walking back toward her barely-conscious victim. "Last, but not least, the fun part." She laughed as she raised the pot and poured boiling, black oil all over Craig. I'd never heard anyone scream like that, and I'd only seen a look of murderous glee like that on one other person — me. The scalding oil peeled Craig's face off from eyebrows to chin and sent it down the drain with inhuman amounts of blood.

"Finish it," I said, lighting a cigarette to mask the smells of shit and piss that Craig reeked of.

"Goodnight, Craig," she said sweetly, dumping two bullets into the back of his head.

Chapter 4

Down to Business

I sat in deep thought, staring at where the three bodies use to be, wondering how it came to be that my baby, my youngest girl, was so much like me even though I'd been gone her whole life. To hear stories about me was one thing, but for her to *be like me* didn't sit well.

"Were those your first kills?" I asked her, noticing her shaking more and more as time went on.

"Uh-huh."

"And now that it's done, how do you feel?"

At first she didn't answer. She simply stared at the wall with unseeing eyes. My initial thought was shock, but it was obvious she was still experiencing coherent thought. It was her emotions that were going wild inside, and sadly I knew she would have to deal with that on her own or be consumed by it.

"I feel," a long, considering pause, "different. Like part of me is just gone, but I don't know if it's the good or bad part. I just murdered three men, one of them was my sister's dad, and I tortured him because he deserved it. He…"

"Deshana, did he…? Please don't tell me that he—"

"It's over, Dad." Silent waves of tears cascaded endlessly down her face. "Daddy, I don't feel regret. I feel alive, and like I finally found the answer to a question I didn't know I'd been asking myself all my life. I'm your daughter, through and through, but there are worse things than that in the world."

I hurt unbearably inside. I hurt for all I'd lost, and I hurt for all my children had lost because they had me for a father. Deep down, I wanted nothing more than to change the past, but since I couldn't, I was gonna make damn sure some people's future was cut short. Starting at the beginning.

"Baby girl, I want you to be better than me in any and every way that you can. I chose the path for my life a long time ago, and I did it this way because I didn't see another way out. You've got a way, sweetheart. Don't let the way I've lived my life steal your joy," I told her, wiping tears from my own eyes. She just looked at me with those big, brown eyes, so dark they looked exactly like my own.

"Daddy, you don't get it. You are my joy. You're all I ever wanted my whole life, and some selfish-ass people took you away from me. I love you, Pop, and we're on this journey together, so whatever happens, happens."

What could I say? I understood why she felt the way she did, but more importantly, I respected it.

"Okay Deshana. Okay."

The door opened and Candy and Keyz came through, followed by three men leading four blindfolded women. Three of the women were strapped to the same chairs as the last victims.

"Give them your chair, Lil' M, and go ahead upstairs." I lit a cigarette, already contemplating who would die first. She gave up her chair so the fourth woman could be strapped down, but instead of leaving, she put a fresh clip in the .44 magnum she had and posted up against the wall.

"Take the blindfolds off and leave," I told the three soldiers, who quickly obeyed my orders and fled. All the women squinted to get their eyes use to the lighting of the room, but recognition dawned clear and instantaneous in three of the four women. "Hello, Monica, Renee, Rebekah. And what's your name, sweetheart?" I asked the terrified young girl sitting closest to me.

"M-mom, what's going on?"

"Devaughn, please don't do this. I'm begging you," Monica whimpered, struggling uselessly against her restraints.

"Keyz, how much time?"

"Three hours, Dee."

"Three. Whole. Hours," I replied, flicking my cigarette at Monica. "Candy, would you kindly relieve these gorgeous women of all their clothing, please?" I stood up and paced back and forth in front of them. I stopped in front of Monica's daughter, raking my eyes across every inch of her shaking body with a mixture of passion and disgust. She was actually quite beautiful with her shoulder-length hair, glossy black, the color of a raven's wings, seductive whiskey-colored eyes, and a voluptuous figure she'd definitely inherited from her mother. I probably could've believed she was mine if it wasn't for her light, coco-butter complexion and obvious Latina heritage.

"Your name?" I asked her again, removing the .45 and dragging it slowly from her breastbone to the delicately-trimmed hair covering her young pussy.

"Devaughn, don't!" Monica cried out, tears falling like rain from behind her glasses.

"Jess. My name is Jessica," she replied, shaking harder by the minute.

"That's a beautiful name, Jessica. Now, do you know who I am?"

"N-no. What do you want with my family?"

"Well, let's do a quick recap, then." I pulled my chair right next to Jessica and rested the barrel of the gun on her thigh.

"Alright, which one of you lying-ass bitches is Renee, and who's Rebekah?" Nobody said anything. The only sounds in the room were Monica's wails and her daughter's equally heavy breathing. "No volunteers?" I stepped in front of the two women whose lies had sentenced me to twenty long, hard years. Quicker than they could blink, I shot the one closest to Monica in the foot. Everyone screamed as the four-pound roared and the black talon tore a clean hole through her little foot.

"I'm Renee," she mumbled, spit and tears landing in a puddle on her lip, wails of agony coming from deep in her stomach when she looked at her ruined foot.

"That makes you Rebekah." I shot her in the kneecap to show my displeasure with her name.

"Devaughn! Devaughn, please, I'll do anything, just leave them alone. I'll do whatever you want me to, please, let them go. It was my fault, my lies," she sobbed, rocking so hard in the chair I thought she would tip over. She was asking for mercy, but I had none to give.

"Tell your daughter the truth, Monica, and I might not kill her."

"Okay. Okay. The truth is that I told this man he was your father to get money out of him. At first I did want to be with him because I saw his potential when it came to making a dollar, but he wouldn't leave his wife. I didn't know what to do. We were living seven-deep in a two-bedroom apartment, you were on the way, and your real father wanted nothing to do with us. I just got so mad! So I — I made my sister lie and say that he touched them and made them suck his dick, and he went to jail."

"You bitch!" Deshana screamed, leaping from the wall and smacking Monica as hard as she could with her pistol. Before I got ahold of her, she hit her again, sending her glasses and a lot of her teeth across the floor.

"Mom!" Jessica yelled, trying to scoot her chair across the floor to console the dazed and bleeding woman.

"I got it, sweetheart, I got it." I set her back on her feet next to Candy and Keyz, who were watching the violence with eyes devoid of emotion. I couldn't blame my daughter for her feelings. She'd finally been told the truth from a source that had no love for her, making the slap of reality that much more painful. This felt wrong. The situation felt wrong because my little girl's pain was in the room, and it was heavy on my shoulders. "Deshana, maybe you—"

"No, Dad, I'm not leaving. Finish what they started." She offering me her razor. The look in her eyes told me she needed to see the end. I needed to know that justice was served.

"I've got something better in mind. Keyz." I held out my .45 and took the scalpel I'd asked her for all those years ago when my plans first started to take form. "You know, Rebekah and Renee, you girls have really grown into some sexy young ladies." I let the light shine brightly on my sharpened instrument of death. "It's almost a shame to waste all this prime, succulent meat."

"Wait — wait, Devaughn," Monica slurred through her broken jaw. I was beyond waiting. I'd waited long enough, and now it was time to really make them hurt. Starting with Rebekah, I cut a Y-incision from both sides of her collarbone all the way down to her shaved pussy and, for good measure, I cut a horizontal line across her stomach. Dropping the scalpel, I reached inside her body and slowly began to pull out her intestines, savoring the look of complete shock and horror on her face. I showed her her body, piece by piece, until she finally lost consciousness, and then I pulled her head back and brutally slit her throat. I heard sharp intakes of breath from behind me while, in front of me, Jessica and Renee threw up. I could tell by the glassy look in Monica's eyes that she had went inside herself and let the shock take away the pain of having to deal with the reality of death surrounding her.

"That is so un-ladylike." I laughed at the two women who were still being violently ill at my feet. "Now, who's next? I'll tell you what, Renee, I've got a proposition for you since it was you who said you sucked my dick repeatedly. Are you a virgin, Renee?"

"Wh-What?"

"Are you a virgin?" Silence. Dead silence. The look of fear in her eyes was loud and priceless, though.

"No. I'm not a virgin," she whispered.

"Good. Candy, get her restraints off her," I ordered, holding out my hand to my sister when she passed me my pistol back.

"Now, Jessica, same question, and I know it'll be hard to answer this in front of your mom, but just think of the consequences if you don't answer," I told her, sitting back in the chair beside her.

"I've — I've masturbated, but I've never actually went all the way before," she replies, blushing hard despite the situation.

"Aww, that's so noble and pure. Now, Renee, I want you to come right over here and kneel in front of me. That's good, I'm glad you're following directions without hesitation. I can tell by the look in your eyes that you think I'm gonna make you do something degrading, like suck my dick? No, not quite. I want you to turn your head to your immediate left, and there you will find your prize." At first she didn't comprehend what I was saying. Then she didn't want to comprehend, but no man or woman's eyes will hide their lies.

"I won't!"

I chambered a round into my gun, grabbed her by her hair, and pulled her so close to Jessica that her pussy hairs were tickling her nose.

"Say it again, bitch, and I'll blow your muthafuckin' head into her stinking-ass pussy," I whispered savagely. Both women cried uncontrollably, wishing for rescue that would never come.

"Aunty. Please," she begged, looking down into Renee's upturned face. Slowly, tentatively, I saw her tongue flick out and shoot in between the silky curls guarding Jessica's virginity. Again, a flick of the tongue and a slight movement of the lips, but it was obvious this bitch thought I was joking with her monkey-ass.

"Lil' M, give me your .44." I moved up behind Renee. "Bitch, you think I'm fucking playing with you?" I screamed, brutally shoving the cold steel of the gun barrel in her asshole, instantly tearing it open. "Shut up your fucking crying and do what I told you," I continued yelling, putting the .45 to the back of her head while cocking the hammer on the .44. Immediately she dove head-first into the pussy, the sounds telling me what I already knew to be true. The look on Jessica's face confirmed my earlier assumption entirely as her head rolled back and her mouth slackened. Her tears were still coming, but now so were the slow moans from deep in her throat. The shaking in her legs told me of the building storm inside her young body as she slightly arched her back, letting her ripe, hard nipples point like two 60mm machine guns toward the sky.

"Oh. Ooh, shit," she rasped.

"Stop," I commanded, withdrawing the pistol from her bleeding asshole and wiping it across her back.

"Wh-What?" Jessica asked, coming back from the edge of the best orgasm she'd never had before into the siege of death and destruction.

"Did you want her to keep going?" I asked the still-blushing young woman before me. Her breathing said yes, her eyes said please, and her body was screaming for somebody, anybody, to do it right just one time.

"Devaughn," Monica croaked, spitting out two more teeth. "Enough. Please let them go."

"Hey, Monica, welcome back. You're just in time to see your baby girl get her first nut from someone other than herself." I pushed Renee out of the way and retook my seat next to Jessica.

"Leave my daughter alone,"

"Leave her alone? Leave her alone? Perhaps the reality hasn't really sunk in for you yet, but I got just the thing for that. Deshana. You see this beautiful young queen standing in front of you, Monica? This is my baby girl, the youngest, and do you know where I've been her whole life? That's right, I've been trapped in a muthafuckin' box. So I ask you, Monica, did you leave my daughter alone? Wait, I guess you did, huh? Because she was without me. Deshana, pull that stinking-ass bitch over here next to her precious daughter."

"Mom!"

"It's alright. I'm here, baby. Everything is alright."

"You know, I told my little girls that same lie for twenty years when they'd cry because I couldn't go home with them. Trust me, a child can always tell a hollow promise. Ain't that right, Jessy?" I taunted, taking my pistol and putting it right at the entrance to her still soaking wet pussy. "And now I'm gonna let you bust that nut." I shoved the gun inside her viciously. I could tell by her screams and the limited movement of the gun that she's been telling the truth about her virginity. Maybe that'd make it easier to get her wings in the afterlife. "Are you watching, Monica?" I asked, grabbing her roughly by her hair without missing a stroke inside her daughter's sweet tightness with my pistol. "Watch," I whispered, angling the gun upward and squeezing the trigger two times. In the wake of Monica and Renee's screams, I pulled the gun out of the stunned Jessica and shot her through the left eye socket, scattering brain fragments across the room. "Kill her." I handed Deshana her pistol back and pulling Renee up by the hair. "Candy, kill her." I handed her my pistol and the sobbing heap of a woman I'd thrown at her feet. Neither woman said a word. They just fired off round after round until all that could be heard in the room was the clicking of empty guns.

I looked into Candy's eyes, searching for any sign of weakness, but all I saw was nothing, the blank stare of a trained killer who'd kill for any reason or no reason. Passing me my gun, she stepped into me, wrapped her arms around and kissed me passionately. I could tell that the kiss meant something, but I was having a hard time analyzing because my body was taking on that familiar heat wave that she caused in me.

"Easy, easy, Candy, we've still got plenty of work to do." Keyz pulled Candy away from me and headed toward the door.

"Where you going, K?" I asked, trying to hold in my laughter. She knew her girl was feeling me in a major way.

"Come on, we've got a meeting to go to, you horny muthafucka," she replied, opening the door and barking out instructions for the disposal of the rest of the bodies.

"Dad?"

"Yeah, sweetheart," I replied, putting my arm around her and leading her out of the room.

"Is that everybody?" The look she gave me was a guarded one, like the question was really more direct than what she was saying, but I gave her the truth anyway.

"Everyone who did me wrong or left me for dead is gonna pay for that, so no, that ain't everybody. Not by a long shot."

She was silent when we boarded the elevator and rode up to the conference room, but I could tell she was in deep thought, so I held her back while everyone else went through the double doors.

"What is it, babe? You know that you can talk to me about anything."

"It's just— I just watched you work down there, and I have a better understanding of you. But after seeing what happens to those who cross you, I can't help except to wonder about mom."

And there it was, the pink elephant in the little ass room. How could I not know that question would come up? She'd just watched me morph into the monster I'd been hiding from her all her life, so how could I tell her I didn't hate her mother in that same way at times.

"I'd be lying to you if I said that killing your mother hasn't crossed my mind a lot in the last twenty years, and to be honest, if you knew the whole story, you might be able to understand why I feel justified. Your mother broke my heart, almost to the point where I committed suicide, but you were what kept me going. I still love your mom a lot, but I hate her about the same amount, too. Look, I don't know what's gonna happen. All I know is that my love keeps me from killing her, and that love is because of you. I was facing eighty-one years in prison, and she didn't have to have you, but she did, and I love her for that." The funny thing about it was that this was the God's honest truth. I still loved the lying, backstabbing bitch, and until I stopped, I doubted my ability to kill her.

"I understand more than you know, Dad, but— Just don't kill her. For me. She's not perfect, but she's the only Mommy I got, and I love her."

I wouldn't make any of my kids a broken promise, and so I took her hand in mine and pushed into the conference room.

When we walked in, Keyz directed toward the head of the table and tossed me my t-shirt back, which I quickly slipped back into. I looked around, immediately sizing up the nine strangers sitting at the table and the two women standing up against the wall.

The room was built like a standard conference room with a mahogony wood table and plush burgandy leather chairs, speaking to the money invested in its decor.

I scrutinized every single individual at the table, making mental assessments before slowly and deliberately putting my pistol back into the waistband of my jeans. It was obvious to me which set was G-Shine because of the trademark sun tattoo on the neck of the man sitting to my immediate left.

The motto of *I Shine, You Shine, We Shine, G Shine* spoke to his rank and identified him as the leader. His face was boyish, and the dimples fitted into his light-skinned complexion made it hard to take him seriously. By comparison, his team was the jungle's finest of lions, tigers, and bears.

The dark-skinned homie sitting next to him was short and stocky, wearing the face only a mother could love. His beady eyes glazed over with obvious hostility and heavy intoxication. The other two brown-skinned niggas next to him could have passed for brothers with identical short haircuts, slight builds, and passive expressions on their faces. I wasn't fooled, though, because dangerous minds hid behind unfocused eyes.

I couldn't deny the beauty of the women accompanying this team of powerful gang members, but they were pretty in a plain sort of way. Both sported short hairstyles and were thick in all the right places, but they were average hood-boogers that were content being that way. No makeup, no sense of style. No thank you.

To my right, the Valentine homies were on their grown-man shit, sporting suites, ties, and fresh gators on their feet. I had known Murder Heart for a while because we had done time together. I almost smiled looking at the huge nose that took up his light-skinned, pimply face. He was a kid who had been the butt of many jokes, but he was a killer, and his eyes always told that story. All his soldiers carried the same look of death in their eyes and determination in the set of their shoulders, each one easily standing six feet, one inch or better, yet graceful with their slight movements.

This round table assortment comprised two of this generation's most powerful Blood sets, but in order to move forward, we had to get some understanding. The price of business was respect. No one's eyes waivered or showed signs of fear, and I liked that.

"Peace, Blood!"

"Peace, Almighty!"

"You niggas know who I am and what I stand for, and your presence here at this round table allows me to draw the conclusion that you represent the same things. With that being said, I appreciate every one of you coming out to welcome me home like real gangstas do. I'm sure you all know my circumstances and situation, but that's the past, and as of now, I'm all about the future of this great movement. I'm sure we all agree that my sister has been more than a capable captain in my absence, and even though I'm home, I still expect business to run smoothly through our territories. So, gentleman, ladies, would you be so kind as to enlighten me on the state of Blood business?" I concluded, sitting down in my seat and accepting the bottle of water Candy handed me.

"First things first, let's make the introductions. Gentlemen, if you please," Keyz said, giving over the floor to our guests.

"More or less, I be dat bloody Murda Heart, five-star General, leader of the Valentine movement for all of Virginia and New York. These four homies to my right are the four one-stars for my line: Black Heart, Creeper, Red Diamond, and Blood Flow," he concluded, retaking his seat. Each man threw up his hood sign as he was introduced, and I acknowledged in kind.

"More or less, I be dat bloody G-Mack, active OG for Shine for the East Coast. The three niggas before you are my five-star Bezo, my three-star Bone, and my two-star Zo Pound. The lovely ladies before you are my two most trusted captains, Red Death and Jewelz." I saluted everyone in his command as well and gave my sister a subtle nod to retake control.

"Now, all three branches of our movement have joined forces for the common cause of making money and providing opportunities in our communities. To date, our collective net worth is somewhere north of $600,000,000 a year, give or take a few million, and that's mainly from our legitimate business ventures. After the recession, we were able to rely more on investment avenues and less on drugs and weapons sales. Now we've pretty much got our hands in everything from local mom-and-pop stores to the new community center we just had built in Petersburg, Virginia. On top of that, business in Texas and North Carolina has improved dramatically in the last eight months thanks to the reinforcements everyone sent to wipe out the opposition.

"I called this meeting for two reasons, ladies and gentlemen," she said, getting up from her seat and walking around the table until she was standing directly behind me with her hands on my shoulders. "One, to inquire about our next business venture or conquest. And two, to make it perfectly clear that my brother will be taking over now that he's home. I want no misunderstanding, because we've all benefited handsomely from our alliance, but *any* question of my brother's authority will not be tolerated. It's because of him that we've been able to thrive as one, and so I believe my demands of respect are reasonable. Do you agree?" she asked the eleven sets of eyes staring at her, pulling my chair back and sitting in my lap. This gave me access to her gun while concealing its view from everyone else.

I could hear the minds of the men working rapidly, weighing out the pros and cons of a war versus continued wealth. A request for respect would've immediately been agreed to without hesitation from any party, but it would not have lasted very long. Respect was never requested, it was demanded at all costs.

"What's your rank, homie?" Bezo asked, something like mild irritation heavily lacing his words when he spoke. My focus wasn't on his words, though. I was studying his body language for any sign of aggression while slowly taking ahold of the pistol at Keyz's back.

"I'm a four-star today, but who knows, I could be a five-star soon," I answered politely, making my threat clear.

"You was a four behind the wall, but I'm asking what your rank is now," he said, not wavering in the slightest. I had two choices, and I knew what they were. This man was questioning me in a blatant, almost disrespectful, way. And to make matters worse his direct superior was sitting right there saying nothing. I took a sip from my water bottle to bide my time and reel in the emotions that were trying to come into play within me.

"Say what you mean and mean what you say, my nigga. In other words, what is it that you really want to ask me? But before you answer, I want you to be mindful of how you talk to me," I told him, my voice only slightly above a whisper. A deadly whisper.

"Be mindful? Nigga, who you are? You might've been some types of big nigga on the inside, but here you're just a little fish in a big pond," he bellowed with malicious laughter. Insults could be tolerated. Laughter? No, that wasn't even in the cards.

"Gentlemen, I'm afraid I'm gonna have to insist that we conclude this meeting for now," I said, calmly setting the water bottle on the table and locking eyes with my daughter, sending her a silent message.

"Aw, what, we not friends no more?" Bezo asked, evoking laughter from the rest of his team.

The first two shots were so close together they sounded like one as Candy and Deshana made quick work of the still-smiling females. Pushing Keyz off my lap, I made equally quick work of G-Mack, Zo Pound, and Bone, training my pistol on Bezo while thoughts of his pistol were still trying to formulate in his mind.

"Murda Heart, this ain't got nothing to do with you or your hood, but all the same, it's probably good that you see this first hand so there won't be any questions later," I said, walking slowly around the table and nodding at my team of two to keep their weapons on the remaining five generals.

"Do you know what you've just done, nigga?" Bezo asked, shaking either from fear, anger, or both.

"What I've done? Yeah, I know exactly what I've done, you stupid muthafucka, but do you?" I questioned, knocking out his two front teeth while forcefully shoving the gun into his mouth. "You couldn't leave it alone, could you? You had to keep pushing when common sense demanded that you just let it go. $600,000,000 a *year*, nigga, and you're worried about my rank? *My rank?*" I yelled, shaking as the rage seeped into me and took over. "You asked who I was, right? Well, nigga, now you know. I be dat bloody nightmare." I pulled the trigger and let his lifeless body fall from my grasp.

"Now." I retook my seat and addressed the silent — and visibly shaken — rest of the committee. "The way I see it is that since we've been in business together this long, it's only fair that I offer you half of Shine's territory for the East, because make no mistake, gentlemen, I fully intend to take it over."

"With all due respect, Dee, you're talking about an all-out war within the movement, and you're not guaranteed victory. You have to observe proper protocol and take these situation to your superiors," Murda Heart replied reasonably. Deep down I knew he was right. My first day home and I'd just started a war separate from the one that was already taking place, but the five dead people on the floor meant I couldn't take it back.

"He's right, Dee." Keyz reclaimed her position in my lap and took the still-smoking gun from my hand. I looked at my daughter and saw the light of understanding clear and steady in her eyes, along with a determination she'd inherited from me and her mother.

"What position will you take when the time for words runs out and street politics is all that remains?" I asked tiredly, the day's events weighing heavily on my shoulders.

"I stand beside you," he replied without hesitation, extending his hand toward me. I took it, signaling that all weapons could be put away for the moment.

"Before we adjourn, I need your help with something. I've got two tons of black diamond I need to unload in a hurry because I've got a batch of some better shit coming in," he said.

"Better than black diamond?" Keyz asked, eyes taking on a glassy look of longing and disbelief.

"Yeah, it's some new hybrid shit from my connections in Europe. Supposedly you can't smoke a whole blunt of the shit, but I'll be sure to send a sample your way," he replied, looking at Keyz with a hunger that I hadn't noticed before now.

"How much?" I asked, wrapping my arms around her protectively, making no mistake to ensure he knew she was off limits. She lay against my chest comfortably, taking my hand in hers.

"For you — $280,000."

Rapidly running the numbers, I calculated my profit, minus what would go up in smoke. "Deal. You can deliver it here sometime today or tomorrow. Keyz, get the man his money." I stood up with her to leave the conference room.

"It was a pleasure doing business," he said as everyone stood and filed past the vigilant Deshana and Candy, who stood guard by the door.

"Now what?" Candy asked when everyone had gone except the three of us.

"Only time will tell what's next to come, but for now I've got a lot of calls to make, and it's already four o'clock," I answered in frustration, gazing at my watch again to make sure it was functioning properly.

"What can I do, Daddy?"

"For now, I need you to go home and spend the night with them to make sure everything's okay. I'm gonna send some people with you, too, but tomorrow everyone — your mother included — has to move out here where I can protect them to the best of my ability. I know school's getting ready to start for all of you, so make sure you tell your sisters to bring everything they need."

"But, Dad, I thought— I thought I was joining you." She crossed to stand in front of me.

"Baby girl, nothing is gonna stop you from getting an education, and I mean that, but, I will allow you to take this one year off and work with me," I replied, kissing her on her forehead.

"Thank you, Daddy."

"You're welcome, now go ahead and get going to the house."

She hugged me tightly and flew out the door before I could change my mind.

"What about me?" asked Candy seductively, walking toward me until she was staring up into my dark brown eyes.

"What's wrong? Are you feeling neglected?" I asked, sliding her onto the table and stepping between her opened legs.

"Just a little. Don't you think it's time we, um, had a private conversation?" she asked, unzipping my pants slowly until she had her prize in the warmth of her palm.

"A conversation, huh? Well, I do believe that I can fit you into my schedule," I told her, claiming her mouth slowly, wanting to savor the sweetness of her tongue as it danced with mine. Her slow stroking motions had me hard within seconds, unbuttoning her jeans and easing them down over her ample hips until they touched the floor. In one motion, I had her panties pulled to the side, and with the first stroke I was in heaven all over again.

"Mmm," she murmured into my mouth, using her hands to pull me deeper into her gooey center and locking her legs behind my back. Every movement was like exploring uncharted territory as the tightness of her pussy walls gave way to new mysteries and hidden treasures. We fit together like a hand and glove, as right as the first biblical scripture, and I was lost in the danger of the woman's wiles.

"Harder, Papi," she demanded, lifting to give me what I was so eager to receive. Pushing her back on the table, I pulled her closer to the edge and wrapped her legs around the back of my neck while I pounded her into glorious submission.

"You muthafuckas are unbelievable!" Keyz screamed, coming through the door and startling both of us.

Behind her stood what I'd come to call the 'body detail', obviously coming to collect the dead people in the room that we had somehow managed to forget. Not ashamed or embarrassed with what I was working with, I pulled my still-glistening hard dick out of Candy and helped her off the table so she could get her pants back on.

"I leave you muthafuckas alone for two minutes to handle business and you're already back at it. Damn, Dee, I said you could fuck her, I didn't say you could have her!" She fixed Candy with a stare that could cut glass.

"It ain't even like that, K," I said, zipping my pants, feeling bad now.

"Oh, ain't it? So then, you won't have a problem never sticking your dick in her again, right?"

"If that's what you want, then say no more about it."

"And you." She turned on a sheepish-looking Candy. "Damn, bitch, is the dick that good?"

"I— It's not like that, baby, I swear. He just— It's just— It won't happen again," She tried to take Keyz's hand, but she shook her off.

"Y'all niggas get these bodies out of here and do something with that truck out front!" she barked at the startled soldiers.

"Dee, you've still got to see your P.O."

"Nah, cancel that shit. I've got three days to see her, and I'm too tired to do shit else today."

"Yeah, I bet."

"Anyway, I'ma just go upstairs and lay down for a while. First I'ma make them calls, and then I'ma relax with a few options, if you know what I mean."

"Yeah, whatever, nigga. Condoms are in the medicine cabinet. You may want to keep some on you, though. We don't want anyone getting pregnant." She looked pointedly at Candy. Common sense was only so common, but I knew not to say anything back.

"Ayo, sis, where all these bodies disappearing to?" I asked, watching the last of my latest victims being carried out.

"I got a crematorium and a funeral home, too," she replied, walking out of the room, leaving me and a visibly-shaken Candy looking after her.

Chapter 5

All Falls Down

It took a while for sleep to come, but when it did, it sucked me down like a body into a fresh grave. I was too spent to fight it after everything that had happened, plus my bath with DC had drained what little energy I did have. My rest was dreamless at first, but when a dream did finally find me, it was so real and sound that I felt like I could touch it.

I was in a room that was unfamiliar to me with a gorgeous female astride me, riding so very slowly. It was like there was no roof whatsoever because I could see the moon and the stars out, but her long, black hair was covering her face. I could feel myself wanting to reach up and cup the enticing, mouth- watering breasts looming over me, but the feeling of her hands on my chest and the mind-bending heat from her achingly slick pussy kept me suspended. It was like time stood still, and we were the only two able to dance to the loving rhythm of give and take. Her moans sounded so real when she picked up speed, going higher and falling farther, taking all of me, yet giving and demanding more still. I felt like I wanted to cum, but how could I? While contemplating this frustrating enigma, my mystery lover rode on, gripping my shoulders and pumping with all her might, chasing or being chased, and I felt my climax well with real need. A blinding light ripped through me as I experience an orgasm like none I'd ever known, frightening me to the point that I screamed out and held onto the bed for dear life.

And just as quickly as the dream had come, it was gone, and I felt myself drifting back into oblivion, nothingness. Falling into the black, my subconscious screamed that something was wrong, but my body demanded sleep, and that's what it got.

When I came to, it was the sound of soft crying that woke me up. At first I thought I was still in prison, but somehow I knew the quiet sobs were entirely feminine and not simply a man who wished he didn't have to be a woman. The moonlight shined brightly, illuminating the whole room, and as I focused on the source of the tears, I found myself looking for DC, but my bed was empty except for a lone figure sitting on the edge of the bed with her shoulders shaking slightly. I didn't know which one of my 'options' this was, so far I'd only been introduced to DC in the biblical sense. I cleared my throat to get her attention, but she didn't turn around.

"Hey, what's wrong, sweetheart?" I asked, voice cracking and alerting me of my thirst. Keyz turned and looked at me with her face covered in tears.

"Keyz." I sat up rapidly, swinging my legs to the edge of the bed. "What's happened? What's wrong? Why are you crying?" I asked, wrapping my arms around her and pulling her closer to me,

"Nothing. It's nothing. I'm just— Oh, Dee, I'm just scared," she mumbled into my chest, clinging to me like a drowning victim. It was then that I realized she had only a t-shirt on and her pistol in her hand.

"What happened, babe? Talk to me." I softly stroked her hair.

"It's just that you just came home, and I don't want to lose you again."

"You're not gonna lose me, Kiara. I'm here, and everything is okay."

"Dee, you've being home one day and so many people have died, not to mention that five of them carry serious repercussions. What if— What if the big homies don't understand? What if they…?"

"Don't think like that, Keyz. Think business-minded. We are part of a $600,000,000 dollar well-oiled machine, and that's not easily expendable."

"But what if they don't care?" she asked, crying harder and holding on tighter to me. I knew her tears were justified because my direct supervisor had been none-too-happy when I told him about a problem that needed to be discussed. He thought, like most rational people did, that I would come home, see the family, and get a little loving in between points A and B. No one in their right mind would've expected thirteen bodies to drop in under eight hours. That was just fucking insane!

"Kiara, do you trust me?" I asked, pulling back so I could gaze upon her beautiful face that was contorted by so much anguish.

"Yes."

"And do you love me?"

"More than you could ever know."

"Okay. That's all I want you to focus on, and let me take care of the rest. I have a meeting at one o'clock tomorrow, and I'll find out then exactly what's gonna happen."

"Am I going to the meeting with you?" she asked, giving me her best puppy dog smile.

"Yeah, you're going with me. Who else would I trust to watch my back at such an important time?"

"I don't know, maybe Candy," she replied, wiping away the last of her tears and fixing me with a look. All I could do was laugh first.

"Listen, babe, Candy is your girl, and I'm not trying to take her from you. Like I said earlier, I won't so much as kiss her again, okay?"

"Bitch thought she was gonna crawl up in my bed tonight. Humph, yeah right. Alright, I know you're gonna leave her alone, but for what it's worth, I can see why she's infatuated with you." She kissed my lips quickly and walked toward the door.

"I told you I was that nigga," I replied, laughing again at the look she gave me before closing the door.

I lay back on the bed, wondering if sleep would find me again, but doubting that possibility. My watch said it was 4:00 a.m., which meant I'd slept for about nine hours, and that was plenty. I could feel the nervous energy flowing through my body in anticipation of today's events unfolding, hoping that I'd still be alive at this time tomorrow.

For some reason my boxers kept sticking to my leg, and that annoyed the shit out of me, causing me to get up and kick them off entirely. I stood at my window naked and watched the creatures of the night make their last preparations before having to surrender to the workers and predators of the day. It was strange to be home, even stranger to be free, but still feel locked up in every sense of the word. Part of me was waiting on count time to be called while I stood at the window until the sun broke the shadows and made its graceful rise to glory. Something inside me was searching for peace, but I'd long since learned that peace could be so elusive that some would consider it a myth. The murders hadn't quenched my thirst for revenge, they had barely sated it, and that made me wonder if any amount of killing would ever lift the crushing weight on my chest. It was my belief that everyone had a little beast in them, and for the right reasons could be provoked to show him. But my beast wasn't normal. He was hungry and demanded to be fed like I demanded oxygen to keep on living. For the most part, I firmly believed I controlled him, but sometimes at night, when the only thing stirring in the world was me and my conscience, I knew deep down who controlled whom.

A brief tapping on my door interrupted my thoughts.

"Yeah," I called without turning around.

"Would you like breakfast brought to you, Mr. Mitchell?" Tara asked, coming into my room.

"What is it?" I asked, turning around to face her, not caring I was naked or that she was staring unashamed.

"What would you like for breakfast?" she asked, licking her lips unconsciously.

"I'll have whatever my sister's having. But what would you like for breakfast, Tara?" I asked, walking toward her until we were inches apart.

"Uh. Excuse— Um, excuse me, Mr. Mitchell?" she said, flustered but somehow managing not to blush.

"When was the last time you were fucked real good?" I whispered, leaning right up against her ear, feeling her shiver at my closeness.

"It's been— Hmm, I don't really recall."

"Well, that's not good. Every woman's body should be cherished and appreciated on a regular basis. Don't you think?" I asked, kissing her neck lightly.

"I do, but— Mmm, but I need this job," she replied, taking a baby step backward, hoping to break the hold I had on her. I could tell she wanted it, maybe even needed it, but she wouldn't sacrifice her position unless I pushed. She was a very attractive woman with shoulder-length brown hair, and her petite frame had the right curves to it, but her best quality by far was the amazing and enchanting gray eyes that were focused on me right now. I could lose myself in her eyes for hours while making love to her body right. She wasn't like these young chicks running around the house. No, I put her as a respectable thirty-two at the most, and she wore it well. I decided I wouldn't push, though. I'd just let her know the door was open.

"You don't have to worry about losing your job on my account." I took her hand in mine. "And when we have sex, trust me, it'll be worth any price asked," I told her, kissing each of her fingers before letting her hand go and walking in my closet to find something to wear.

"Promises, promises," I heard her say as she left the room in a hurry, and I couldn't help laughing at what just happened.

I was turning into a sex-crazed madman! It was time to slow down and get focused, because today could very well be the beginning of the end. I felt like dressing business casual today as I selected some tan Gucci slacks, an all-white button-up, and some tan gators to set off the ensemble. I took a quick shower and was just putting on a touch of cologne when one of my favorite smiling faces bent around the corner of my bedroom door,

"Hey, pretty lady." I stood and gave Keyz a bone-crushing hug.

"Oh, Dee, damn." She laughed and struggled to get loose.

"Well, you look a lot better now than at four this morning, no offence."

"None taken, smartass, but I do feel better thanks to you. I'm glad you were there when I needed you."

"No problem, Light Skin, you know I got you. But I do have one question: where's my suitcase?"

"Damn, my bad, bruh. I had Tara put everything in the safe while we handled that little business. The safe is in your closet on the back wall, and the combination is your birth date."

"How many people know about this safe?" I asked, going in, opening it, and taking out $20,000 plus the baby Uzi and the extra clip.

"Just me, you, and Tara, but don't trip, because I trust her. And why are you smiling like that?" she asked, watching me when I came out of the closet stuffing money and the extra clip in my pocket.

I didn't answer right away. I just gave her my best innocent look.

"Aw, come on, Dee, don't tell me you fucked her that quick!" She was clearly frustrated by my choice to interfere with a valued employee.

"Nah, nah, she just came in while I was naked and things almost got out of hand. She's loyal to us, though, so I'm not gonna pursue her."

"Please don't. Listen, my nigga, I understand you went twenty years without no pussy, but damn, you ain't gotta stick your dick in everything that's willing to have you! Your shit gonna fall off, and then what? You gonna be looking stupid. You got five chicks right down the hall ready to worship you like the black Hue Heffner. Come on, stop the bullshit. Haven't you learned anything about playing with a woman's emotions?"

I couldn't argue with the truth. I was trying to fuck everything that wasn't nailed down, and some things that were. It wasn't just about pussy, though. I wanted real love. But right now I was focused on what had to be done today in order for me to be alive to chase that dream.

"You're right. So, what's on your agenda for today?"

"Well, I gotta swing past two of my beauty salons and see what business looks like, then I gotta go to the car dealership and see when my new ride will be ready. I got a holographic business meeting at 11:00 a.m. with some Tokyo investors who want me to get in on this new computer chip shit they got going on. First thing I'ma do, though, is shoot over to the boys' and girls' club in west VA. You remember the one you use to go to?"

"Yeah."

"Well, I be going out there every few weeks to make sure everything they need is available. I just sent twenty new computers up there, so I need to make sure everything is straight. After my meeting, it's me and you. So, what you gonna do?"

"I gotta go holla at Mikko and get them moved out here A.S.A.P. I was thinking about putting them in the small house, if that's cool with you?"

"Yeah, I'm alright with that, but you know you gonna end up fucking Mikko, right?"

"Fuck outta here," I told her, smiling despite my efforts not to. "Anyway, after I go out there, I'ma slide through and see my P.O.

real quick and get that shit out of the way. Once that's done, I'ma be here until you get back."

"Sounds like a plan, my nigga. Let's get something to eat and get to it." She turned to walk out the door.

"Question?" I said, slinging the gun over my shoulder and following her.

"What's that?"

"What am I driving?"

"Oh damn, I'm really buggin'. That's my fault, I forgot to tell you that I copped you a 2020 Navigator, and that bitch is tricked out like my Benz. Black on black, sitting on all-black twenty-six-inch rims, but it ain't the regular factory size, because I had them make it longer so your privacy window could be installed. Plus you got a driver, but you can't — I repeat, *cannot* — fuck her, Dee, under any circumstances."

We took the elevator down and I contemplated who my driver could be, my curiosity getting the best of me in the worst way. For her to say I absolutely couldn't fuck her for any reason meant only one thing in my mind: this chick was bad!

"Who is it?" I asked, following her into the kitchen.

"Be patient, she should be here any minute, but I'm telling you that the girl is hands-off, or I'ma fuck you up personally."

"Bitch, please, you know you can't beat me," I pinned her to the counter and tickled her until she couldn't catch her breath.

"Alright, damn! You play too much. What kind of cereal do you want?"

"Now, see, that's what I'm talking about. I knew you still had some hood in you, despite all the money and this big-ass house out here in the suburbs."

"Fuck you, nigga." She laughed and grabbed two big bowls that were supposed to be used for cake mixing.

"I know you got some Captain Crunch with the crunch berries." I took the milk from the refrigerator and pulling out one of the stools at the island in the middle of the kitchen.

"My nigga, I got every kind of Captain Crunch," she replied, going into the pantry and coming out with two identical boxes. Handing me mine, a spoon, and a bowl, we got down to business like a couple of four-year-olds who had no time for games. Cereal has always been one of my favorite things to eat, but the opportunities for it in prison were few and far between. I never actually realized how much I missed the little things until they were taken from me.

"So, what's your girl gonna do while we handle business?" I asked around a mouthful of crunch berries.

"I don't know, but that's a good question." She set her spoon down and tipped her bowl up to get the rainbow-colored milk.

"Ugh, slurping and shit." I followed her lead.

"Intercom on. Page Candy to the kitchen." Immediately following that, I heard a ding like an airport loudspeaker before a voice told Candy to make her way to the kitchen directly.

"This shit is too much." I shook my head, getting up to put my bowl in the sink and the remains of the cereal back in the pantry. Coming back out, I pulled up short at the sight of a modern-day version of Pocahontas, utterly intoxicating in her skin-tight blue jean shorts, blue and white Air Force Ones, and a white t-shirt that said *So good at being bad*. Only a little shorter than Keyz, she had the most perfect sun-kissed brown skin, free of any blemishes, with long, sexy eyelashes accenting her penetrating almond-shaped gray eyes that seemed to be evaluating me as I was her. Wiping my face to ensure I didn't have an embarrassing milk mustache, I stepped forward to introduce myself.

"How are you doing, beautiful? I'm Dee." I extended my hand.

"I know who you are," she replied, her voice effortlessly sensual as she continued to hold me captive with her eyes. One thing Mikko had taught me was eye contact, especially when making love.

"Dee, this is Eternity, Tara's daughter." Keyz separated my hand from hers and stepping in front of me so she could give me the evil eye.

"Daughter? How old are you?" I asked, ignoring my sister completely.

"I just turned eighteen last week."

"Congratulations. I'll have to be sure to get you something special for the occasion."

"Nah, nigga, you not gonna give her shit," Keyz whispered fiercely, pushing me backward a few steps and signaling for the girl to hold on. "Listen, I already told you no, muthafucka. She's gonna drive you around, that's it. Not ride you, not suck you, just drive, Dee! Come on, nigga, don't do it. Don't fuck up this girl's life."

That statement got my attention, and I finally looked at her, knowing the hurt was shining brightly in my eyes.

"Fuck her life up? That's what you think of me, Kiara?"

"No, I didn't mean it like that."

"Yeah, whatever." I picked up the gun off the kitchen counter and turned around as Candy walked into the kitchen.

"Let's go, Eternity." I walked out of the kitchen and past Candy without saying a word.

"Dee, what?"

"Leave him alone," I heard Keyz say. I never checked to see if the young girl was following me. I just assumed the obvious, opening the front door and stepping out into the bright morning sunshine. My truck was parked right in front of the house, behind the shining Benz, and despite my anger, I had to grudgingly admit that she'd done a good job. Walking around the vehicle, I did a quick inspection and couldn't help but smile when I looked at the license plates. She'd somehow managed to get diplomatic plates with nothing other than "EMU" printed on it. I loved her beyond reason, but her comments had hurt me. Even more infuriating was the realization that she could hurt me. That said a lot.

"Dee, I don't know exactly what that was all about back there, but I know it had something to do with me," Eternity said, walking up next to me and opening my door.

"Do you wanna know what it was about?" The look on her face said yes, but I guess she didn't know if more trouble would be caused by her curiosity, because she didn't respond. I stood there staring at her until she was forced to look away from my intense and powerful gaze.

"You're a very beautiful young woman, but I'm sure you already know that. The argument between my sister and I was her wanting me to keep our relationship professional."

The explicit meaning behind my statement caused her eyes to snap back to mine, but the message in them was unclear to myself, probably as much as it was to her.

"Me personally, I'd like to make sweet love to you from the tips of your fingers to the depths of your soul, and then awaking and do it all over so you never forget the taste of me for the rest of your life," I said huskily. "But that's just me," I told her, smiling at the astonished look on her face while I climbed into the truck. After a moment, my door closed and I heard her climb behind the wheel.

"Where to?" she asked, lowering my privacy window just enough to allow me to see her eyes, I gave her the address to Mikko's house, and we were off down the highway. Like a kid with a new toy, I explored my truck, opening up compartments and finding a bar stocked with my favorites, along with packs of Dutches.

"Okay, I got the blunts, but where's my weed?" I wondered aloud.

"Did you say something?" she asked, lowering the window more until her gorgeous face came into view.

"I'm looking for my smoke."

"Oh, it's in the armrest right there in the middle, and there's another two ounces in the hidden compartment if you run out."

Searching where she said, I found a healthy sandwich bag of sticky, a pack of cigarettes, a lighter, and the remote for my T.V. Now all I had to do was find the T.V.

"Buttons are in the door panel." She read my mind exactly. A thirteen-inch flat-screen dropped out of the sky, and I turned it to the news while I cracked a blunt and rolled up my morning fix. I was searching for news of the residential shooting yesterday, but nothing came up, which allowed me to breathe a sigh of relief. That hadn't been the craziest move yesterday, but there was no way I was gonna lead them to the spot my kids rested at. I forgotten to ask Keyz if them niggas had turned up yesterday. I definitely wanted to eliminate them before this latest issue got started.

I found myself in deep thought about the pending war and its ramifications while the powerful marijuana crept into the corners of my brain and spoke comforting truths. I couldn't really predict how things could turn out, and that bothered me, because normally when I applied my mind to a problem, the solution manifested sooner rather than later. Hopefully my meeting later went well, because the support of my hood meant more than anyone else who had my back.

"Can I ask you a question?" she said, snapping me out of my internal struggles.

"Yes."

"Did you mean what you said earlier — about making love to me?"

Those eyes were direct and unwavering, her voice strong, and she wasn't blushing in the slightest. I evaluated all this silently, taking long, lazy draws on my blunt. "I always say what I mean. Why? Did I offend your young sensibilities?"

"Age had nothing to do with it. You don't strike me as a man who bullshits, meaning when you want something, you most likely get it. I just want to know why you wanna make love to me?" she asked, lowering the window completely now.

"Initially it was purely based on the physical, but now I'm more intrigued by you than anything. There's something about you that says you're not the average empty-headed eighteen-year-old concerned with shoes or the latest fashions, but you know what it is."

"Oh, I'm way more than that, but I've never met a man who wanted to make love to me before. I have a feeling that you know how to fuck, but to make love you'd actually make it about me and not yourself."

"And does that speak to you?" I asked, finishing my blunt and lighting a cigarette.

"I'm not gonna lie, you're a sexy nigga, but my thoughts run more along the lines of what happens the morning after?"

"Honestly, that would depend on two things. One, how good you are, and two, what promises you'd be asking me to make you."

My honesty might have been too much for her, because she didn't answer right away, leading me to believe the conversation was over. It didn't bother me. Like Keyz told me, I had pussy every which way I turned, so I ain't really have to go looking.

The rest of the ride was made with only the sounds of the morning news to keep me company. When we pulled up in front of Mikko's house, I realized I'd made a mistake by not bringing a pistol, and I couldn't exactly hop out with an Uzi over my shoulder. This wasn't the Congo.

"You got a gun?"

She held up the chrome and wood handle like it was a starter pistol.

"Any guns on board?"

"Hit the switch on the door panel marked cops," she replied, putting the truck in park and getting out. I hit the button and the seat in front of me that was facing me lifter up. Looking down inside, I found my two HKMP5s with plenty of clips for them and the baby Uzi, as well as two glock .40s and a Taurus 9mm. I put the Uzi and extra clip in and took out one of the glocks, loading a thirty-two-shot clip in and chambered my first round. Quickly putting it in the waist of my pants, I stepped out of the truck when she opened my door.

"Where are you hiding that big-ass cannon?"

"Don't worry, I got it," she replied, smiling seductively. I started to move her, but she stopped me by grabbing my hand. "There's a cop car with two people in it fifty feet to your left." She laced her arms on my neck as if to kiss me.

"Okay, we'll be in and out as quick as possible. Back the truck into the space right there and be ready for anything. When you get back in, I want you to get the HK from out of the seat," I replied, nuzzling her neck affectionately and enjoying the feel of her body.

"And just so you know," she gazed into my eyes, "I want you to make love to me."

"I know," I whispered, pulling away from her and walking up the stairs.

I didn't bother knocking this time. I simply opened the door and called, "Daddy's home!" loud enough for the neighbors to hear.

"Nigga, what you doing walking in my house?" Mikko asked with serious attitude.

"Hello to you too, lovely. Where's everyone?"

"Sleep. What, you don't do that anymore?"

"Why are there two cops watching your house?"

"Because Craig is missing. Or didn't you know?" she asked, her eyes relaying the implication in her words clearly.

"Missing persons cases take twenty-four hours to file, I just saw the nigga yesterday, so how the fuck are the police on this quick?"

"Craig was an informant," she replied hesitantly.

"You laid up in here with a snitch?" I was enraged, not able to keep my voice down.

"It's not like—"

"What's up, daddy?" Deshana said, coming down the hall with a suitcase in her hands.

"Don't worry," I said, giving her a hug and a kiss.

"Where you's going?" Mikko asked quickly.

"Come on, Mom, don't start, because I already told you that we're all going to Aunt Kiara's house."

"I ain't going no—" She was caught midsentence by the knock at the door.

"Who is it?" she called out, looking at me.

"Detective Holloway, ma'am." With a smile on her face, she got up to open the door. Being far from stupid, I took the glock and gave it to Deshana who quickly put it in the waist of her jeans. The door opened and two cops entered, both with their hands on their weapons.

"Is everything alright, ma'am?"

"Fine, officers. What can I do for you this fine morning?"

"I was just wondering if we could have a word with your husband here."

"Ex husband," she corrected quickly.

"Right, ex husband."

"I got two words for you, officer: *Dale Race*. That's the name of my attorney. So feel free to contact him at your earliest convenience if you want to talk," I told them, smiling as nicely as I could.

"Lawyer already?" Didn't you just get out yesterday, Mr. Mitchell? What need do you have for an attorney?"

I responded by calling out my attorneys phone number.

"I'm gonna be watching you, Devaughn." The detective stepped into my personal space. "You keep your finger on speed-dial, because I'm gonna be watching you, and the first time you fuck up, you're going back inside."

I knew he was hoping to provoke me, but I wouldn't give him the pleasure.

He knew he couldn't touch me, couldn't so much as search me, but what made it worse is he knew that I knew he couldn't do shit. One thing criminals were guaranteed to learn on the inside was their rights, always quick to tell a C.O. they were gonna give them what they deserved.

"Ms. Jackson, you have a nice day," the officers said, retreating the way they'd come, and still watching me every step of the way. Once the door closed, he looked at Mikko with the hunger of a predator eyeing his next meal.

"Dad?"

"Un-uh, just you and your sisters get your shit, and let's go," I told her, feeling the anger surging through my viens, begging to be released.

"But, Dad, what about mom?" she asked, her voice breaking slightly, causing me to look at her. The minute I did, my anger vanished as fast as it had come, and I just wanted to take the pain out on my baby's eyes.

"Mikko, will you please come with us?" I asked as humbly as I possibly could.

"What about Craig?" she asked, her eyes challenging me with blatant accusation.

"I don't know anything. I promise you, I didn't harm him in any way, nor did I order it done," I told her truthfully. Out of the corner of my eye, I could see Deshana shift uneasily. I could tell Mikko was weighing my words very carefully, searching my eyes for the truth she believed was hidden just below the surface.

"It's gonna take me a while to pack up Jordyn and Nick, but I'll go if that's what you think is best."

"I do."

"Fine, give me a few hours and come back." She headed for the stairs to begin the arduous task of packing for an uncertain length of time.

"You named him Nick?"

My question stopped her in her tracks, sending both of us spiraling into the past. Our families had known each other a long time, almost since before our births. At one point in life I thought that proved us destined to be together. Nick, AKA Boobie, was my friend and her cousin who was lost in a terrible car accident a long time ago. Gone, but not forgotten.

"After Boobie," she said and kept walking up the steps.

"Thank you, Daddy," Deshana said, flinging herself into my arms.

"Anything for you, sweetheart, anything. Now, give me my gun back. Wait, you still got one, right?"

"Yeah, I got the glock .19, and I still got the .44, but I washed it because it smelled like shit." She frowned her beautiful pug nose at me. I made no reply to that as she handed me my gun back and I put it in my pants.

"Alright, look, your backup is still outside, so what I want you to do is stay here and wait on everybody, then bring them to the house. I got some other important business to handle, but I'll meet you all later on." I kissed her on her forehead and opening the door.

"Be safe, Dad."

"You too, baby."

"Everything good, Eternity?" I asked, climbing in the back and reaching for the cellphone.

"Yeah, they're back in their car, and I haven't seen any more yet."

"That's good, that means their backup hasn't arrived, so let's get out of here," I told her, listening to the phone ring until Keyz picked up.

"Yo."

"Find out everything you can on a Detective Holloway, Fairfax P.D., and just so you know, Craig was an informant, so check into that, too,"

"Got it," she replied, disconnecting.

"Are they following us?" I asked, hitting the button to open up the gun chest again,

"Nah, it doesn't look like it, but by now they should've seen the diplomatic plates on this bitch," she replied, pressing hard on the gas when we bent the corner, leaving the neighborhood. A quick look at my watch showed it was 11:00 a.m. already. Damn, where did the time go?

"Look, I gotta see my P.O.," I told her, running off the address and sticking the pistol back in the stash. I couldn't walk into the courthouse with a gun, anyway. I rolled another blunt and put it in the air, letting my mind turn over the fact Craig must have been more worried about imminent death than anything else. It was still hard to believe Mikko sank so low as to fuck with a nigga like him. I wasn't a million-dollar nigga when I left, but my potential was limitless, and she knew that. The only thing Craig had been destined for was a painful death.

The drive to Fairfax was a short one, and before I knew it, I had to put my blunt out and face the music.

"Keep your eyes open," I said, hopping out and making the short walk to the building. After passing through the metal detectors, I took the elevator up to the third floor where I met a grandmotherly-type receptionist.

"May I help you, young man?"

"Yes, I'm here to see Ms. Ramona Petras."

"Down the hall, second door on your left, room 305."

"Thank you." I turned and followed her directions until I came to the correct spot. I knocked twice and was told to enter. Nothing could've prepared me for what awaited me on the other side of the door as I opened it and came face-to-face with a beauty that rendered me speechless. Curly jet-black hair, smooth tanned skin the color of hot chocolate, eyes as black as night with a mouth that formed the sexiest pout I'd ever seen, all nicely complimented by a voluptuous figure hugged tightly by a bright yellow summer dress. My eyes travelled, making all this once and then again, only stopping the third time because the tone of her "May I help you?" had changed from sunny to ice cold.

"I'm so very sorry. I don't know what came over me just now. I'm not normally so awestruck by beauty, but damn, you're amazing."

"Thank you. Really, can I help you?" she asked again, this time not as hostile, and I could tell she was trying to suppress a smile.

"Yes, um, I'm looking for Mrs. Ramona Petras."

"Yes, Miss Petras, and that's me," she replied, extending her hand.

"Nice to meet you, I'm Devaughn Mitchell." I took the offered hand, but noticed a chill creep into her eyes at the mention of my name,

"Well, nice of you to show up, Mr. Mitchell, but I was expecting you yesterday."

"I apologize, the family reunion ran a little over, and for once I lost track of time."

"Understandable. However, now I have a prior engagement." She closed the door behind her.

"Okay. Um, would you like me to schedule an appointment?" I asked, following her to the elevator, feeling like a fifteen-year-old with a crush and hating myself for it.

"Well, if you see my receptionist, I'm sure she will fit you in at my next available slot."

"How about lunch today?" I asked, stepping on the elevator with her.

"Lunch? Like a date? No. Sorry, that would be quite inappropriate, I'm afraid."

"Ms. Petras, I'm good at keeping secrets. Besides, it's not a date if we go Dutch."

"I really can't." She walked out of the elevator and the courthouse with me hot on her trail.

"Hold up for a second." I caught her in front of my truck. "Look, before you knew my name, would you have gone out with me?"

"I don't know. Maybe, but it doesn't matter, ok? I do know now."

"Listen, sweetheart, I'm not saying have my baby. All I want is—"

"Dee, look out!" Eternity screamed. It wasn't until then that I heard the sounds of a V8 engine roaring as tires squealed and automatic gunfire shattered the morning's peaceful nature. Instincts kicked in, forcing me to push Ramona toward the protection of the truck as I caught the HK being thrown to me and spun toward the idling car with murder on my mind. I pumped shell after shell at the now-moving targets of the two men hanging out of car windows, praying I hit the gas tank or at least the driver. Sensing the fight was over, my flight instincts kicked in. I'd just engaged in gun battle in the middle of a city that was known for one thing and one thing only: police. Turning around to jump in the truck, I noticed the bleeding woman three feet from me. Unwilling to leave her, I scooped her up in my arms and, with as much care as speed would allow, put her in the truck.

"Drive this muthafucka!" I screamed, checking for how many bullet holes the unconscious Ramona had in her. My first search only shower a flesh wound, but a closer inspection showed one in her side, and it was bleeding with a vengeance. "Fuck," I yelled, grabbing my cellphone while trying to keep as much pressure on the wound as possible. "Keyz, we got a problem. Niggas tried to hit me coming out of my P.O.'s office."

"Are you hurt?" she asked, worry lacing every word.

"No, but my P.O. is, and I got her with me."

"What the fuck, Dee?"

"I don't know what she saw, Kiara, because I was shooting back! We just turned Fairfax into a goddamn war zone, and I wasn't about to risk her statement to the police. Now get a doctor, because I'm on my way."

"Hurry," she replied, disconnecting the call.

"Eternity, listen to me, babe. I need you to drive this motherfucking vehicle like your life depends on it, okay?" I saw her shake her head, and I knew she was too shocked to talk. All I could do was look at the still, almost angelic face of the woman whose blood was pumping through my fingers, willing her not to die. If she died, they'd hang it on me. And then they'd hang me. Whatever plan I had up until now just went out the window.

The inevitable had happened.

It was war.

Aryanna

Chapter 6

Raw

The next forty-eight hours passed in a whirlwind of activity with me at its core, but I hardly noticed. I felt like a schizophrenic patient with thousands of personalities and voices in my head, because everyone had an idea or opinion on how to handle the situation. All I could think was too many chiefs and not enough Indians, but I said nothing and just smoked blunt after blunt while keeping a visual over Ramona. Eternity may have been young, but she knew how to handle that truck, and luckyily we'd made it in time for Ramona's life to be saved. Barely.

Knowing that more often than not hospitals would be off limits, Keyz had the good sense to buy a surgical team that she kept on standby. Looking at the still unconscious woman sleeping in my bed, I was thankful that my sister somehow managed to think of everything, because if she hadn't, this woman could've died.

I shivered just thinking about what would come next. As it was, I still didn't know what would happen, but knew my chances increased dramatically as long as she was still breathing. I'd only left her side a few times in the past two days, to get my kids and their mom settled and turn the house into an impenetrable fortress. The potent smoke of the marijuana didn't mask the smell of the dried blood that stained my clothes and my still-shaking hands. My hands didn't shake in fear, but in anger. I'd heard stories about people being so mad all they could see was red, but all I saw was black. All I had eyes for was death. Admittedly, I didn't have a clear plan, but there was no way I'd willingly accept the role of the hunted without mounting some type of defense. I'd earned the stripes I wore and the rank I claimed proudly, and I stood behind my decisions of those who'd perished at my hand since I'd come home. My frame of mind now was *fuck anybody who didn't agree.*

Finishing my blunt, I stepped to the side of the bed and simply gazed upon the beauty of her, but it wasn't lust that flooded my mind. It was longing. She was showing incredible strength fighting for her life, and that made me want to know about her. What was she clinging onto so tightly that allowed her to keep going when her body had demanded she stop? She had stories to tell, and I wanted to hear them, but I wasn't sure if I had the right to ask for that privilege. What made me entitled to her or her world? In her eyes, I was simply a criminal who was back on the streets for a limited amount of time, and in a lot of ways I had to agree with that assessment. She couldn't know or understand that the one thing I longed for more than freedom during those twenty years was the most elusive thing for any person: love.

"She still ain't woke up yet?" Keyz whispered, entering the room quietly.

"Nope. What's the latest report?"

At this question, she signaled me to follow her toward the bathroom, where she closed the door to avoid eavesdropping.

"Bad news. You're wanted for questioning with the shooting and disappearing act that we pulled with sleeping beauty. No warrants have been issued, but witnesses say a stocky black male, approximately five-ten or five-eleven in height with close-cut wavy hair was seen shooting at the fleeing car. Your clothing was described, but when pictures of you were shown, nobody was 100 percent. One of the two shooters ended up dead a few blocks away, but amazingly everybody else got away."

"What kinda car was it?"

"Eternity says it was a burgundy Audi, a 2014 Model."

"License plates?"

"You're not gonna like it. They said Julius B. What do you want to do?"

I summed up her report mentally, but I was only able to draw one conclusion: I was fucked. There was no way I could go to the police willingly for questioning with Ramona still unconscious, but ducking them would mean they'd come looking for me. On top of that, I had to strategize my move against the niggas who'd tried to get me and basically conduct a war right under the noses on the authorities.

"What's Skino say?"

"He said he wants to see you now, and that he expects you in Tidewater in the next twenty-four hours."

I definitely didn't like the sound of that command, but when a superior said come, the underlings came, no questions.

"What time is it?" I asked, looking down at my clothing in disgust, yearning for a hot bath.

"It's a little after 5:00."

"A.m. or p.m.?"

"Damn, big bro, is it that bad? I know you can see all this sunshine behind you," she replied, gripping my face in her hands and checking my eyes.

"My bad, sis, I'm trippin'. I'ma take a bath real quick as I get my mind right. Tell Eternity to be ready to leave by 9:00 p.m., and tell Candy to be ready, because I'm taking her with me."

"Wait a minute, nigga, I'm coming, too!"

"Listen, you gotta stay here and hold the fort down." I took her face in my hands. "There's no way I can leave this house or everything that you worked so hard for unprotected. I need you to trust me, sweetheart, and right now I need you to be my backbone. You're all I got, for real," I told her, wiping her tears away and kissing where they use to be.

"But, Dee— Please." She clasped my hands that still held on to her beautifully innocent face. I knew it was fear that was talking as much as it was the love she had for me. It was funny, how we didn't grow up together, but she was my everything, and I hated to see the pain and hurt she was in. I couldn't take the chance, though. I had to present myself alone and be prepared to deal with whatever consequences would be because of my actions. Kissing her gently on the forehead, I released my hold on her, opened the door, and made my way to my closet for fresh clothing. I could hear her leave the room hesitantly, but the time for coddling had passed. She was a big girl, and this was real shit, and it was time to face the reality.

Opening my safe, I put ten of the $20,000 I'd taken back in and closed it. Next I picked out an all-billionaire Armani suit, black shirt, gray tie, and matching gray gators as my outfit to "meet my maker," so to speak. I dropped the clothes across the end of my armoire and hopped in the shower. The hot water worked its magic on my bones and screaming muscles, relaxing me to a degree that allowed me time to clear away some of the clutter in my brain. When I stepped from beneath the spray, my thoughts finally had some much-needed organization and direction, but I still knew my battles would be many before I was allowed to rest.

Back in the room, I saw Candy standing as the foot of my bed, silently watching Ramona, but her thoughts were guarded by the blank look in her eyes.

"What's up, Red?"

"Why'd you bring her here, Dee? Why didn't you leave her in the streets to die?" She spoke softly, but the venom in her voice was unmistakable, and unless I missed my mark, so was the hostile jealousy.

"Because she didn't deserve to die like that, and if I had let her die, who do you think they would've hunted?"

"They're hunting you anyway." Her eyes shone bright when she looked at me, and I began to realize what I thought was just a casual sexual relationship. There was something I missed.

"You wanna know something?" she asked softly.

"Okay."

"I'd only been with one other guy before you. One. And after him, I only dealt with women, because he hurt me in a way that most women are sensitive to. Have you ever had your heart broken, Dee?"

"Yeah."

"So then, you know how it is to put yourself back together afterward. I somehow managed to put myself back together, and I've been doing fine, Dee. I love your sister very, very much, but I wish— I wish she hadn't told me everything about you to the point where I felt like I knew you before we met. I wish she didn't let us sleep together, because now that's all I can think about."

She fell silent after these declarations, leaving me searching for words to fill the void, but I had none. I knew what she was trying to tell me, and more than anything part of me liked the way she felt about me, but the time wasn't right.

"Candy—"

"Don't." She held up her hands to silence whatever she anticipated my next statement to be.

"Keyz said you wanted to see me."

"Uh. Yeah, we're leaving for Norfolk at 9:00, and I need you to go with me. I don't know what the situation's gonna be like when we get there, so be prepared for anything."

"Ready." She turned and left the room. Trying to push all thought from my mind, I got dressed quickly, realizing I still had to go to the other house and check on everyone.

"She obviously loves you," came a weak voice from behind me, startling me and causing me to reach for a gun that wasn't there.

"How long have you been awake?" I asked her, moving to and sitting on the side of the bed.

"Water?"

I uncapped the bottle and helped her take a few healthy swallows before putting it back on the nightstand.

"Better?"

"Mm, thank you."

"So, you heard that whole conversation, huh?"

"I heard what she said and what she didn't, and I'm guessing so did you."

"Yeah, but I'm not exactly a good person to love right now. You talking to me almost got you killed."

"And from what I understand, your life would have been easier if you'd let me die. So why didn't you, and how about the real reason this time?"

"Those were my real reasons, plus I'm sorry you saw me shooting back, and I was afraid of what you might say."

"Ah, and now the whole picture comes into focus. If I ask you, will you tell me what happened, or rather why it happened?"

Looking into her eyes. I searched for a trust I had no right to expect from her, but my gut told me it was there. "How familiar are you with my file?"

"Let's see, I know why you went to prison, although it's completely uncharacteristic with your criminal history. I know that while you were in they tried to tie you to several different gangs until you finally chose one, so I guess that makes you a gangbanger."

"I prefer street revolutionary political soldier. Gangbanger is so 1980s."

"As you wish, but either way, you're into some heavy shit, and for people to be taking shots at you in front of the courthouse, I'm willing to bet that's what it's about."

"Well, Ms. Petras—"

"Ramona. Considering I'm laid up in your house and you saved my life, I guess we're on a first name basis."

"Fine, Ramona, if you're a betting woman, then you just hit the lottery. I can't give you specifics, but let's just say a few people ain't happy I'm home. What I really need to know is how is this gonna play out in your official report?"

Her black eyes stared at me, almost to the point where I felt like she was looking through me. I didn't feel an unease that one would normally feel under such scrutiny, but more so something close to calm, because I had the sense I was being judged as a man, nothing more, nothing less.

"I'll do what I can, to see that you don't go back to prison for anything that has to do with this, but my question for you is what difference is it gonna make? They're gonna gun you down anyway." It was a very real question, and it damn sure wasn't out of the realm of things that could possibly happen in the very near future. Truthfully, I wasn't worried about dying. The only men who were scared to die were those who hadn't lived.

"Let me worry about that," I told her, standing up and brushing my suit off."

"Okay, have it your way. Where are my clothes so we can get going?"

"Going where?"

"You're taking me home." She grimmaced in pain when she tried to move.

"First of all, stop moving before you open up your wound. You were lucky as hell to survive with all that shit that bullet hit inside you. Don't press your luck. Secondly, you can't go home."

The fire in those black eyes was instantaneous, bringing much-needed color back to that sexy face in a rush.

"What do you mean, I can't go home?"

"What I mean is, you were a witness to an attempt made on my life. How long do you think you'll live before someone comes to silence you permanently? We have a strict no-witness policy."

"But that's bullshit!"

"I understand how you feel, but your face has been plastered all over the news, and you're wanted for questioning. Look, just give me seventy-two—"

"It's worse than that, Dee," Keyz said, coming in, grabbing the remote off of the nightstand, and pushing buttons to raise the T.V. out of the chest at the foot of my bed. As soon as she turned the T.V. on, I saw my own face looking back at me. I was stunned to the point where I couldn't focus on shit they were saying. They just kept showing video of me and Ramona walking out of the courthouse, and moments later the reactions inside when automatic guns ripped through the air. Then they cut to a cul-de-sac that looked vaguely familiar, but I couldn't place it.

"—what I'm saying?"

"Huh?"

"Now do you see what I'm saying?" Keyz asked me again.

"No."

"Dee. The shells found in that neighborhood match some of the ones found yesterday, and being that Mikko stays right there, they're no longer trying to question you. They're using words like "suspicion" and giving out numbers to call. Nigga, shit's serious."

I didn't know what to say. This was the last thing I needed right now. I knew I couldn't lose my composure.

"Did you get in another shooting?"

"Not now, Ramona."

"Did you?" she persisted, trying in vain to sit up.

"What do you want from me, huh? You want me to tell you that I'm the shit bad dreams are made of? Fine, that's what it is. The sad truth is that I live in a horror movie where the end is so predictable that everyone is just waiting on the credits to roll. If my enemies don't get me first, then the police will."

"Dee?"

Only one thought crossed my mind when I looked from the disapproving look Ramona was throwing to Keyz's unanswered questions, and only one conclusion made sense.

"I'm all in. Call our soldiers and get them up here for a meeting in two hours, and call you-know-who and tell him that I'll be there, but I think it's safer if we don't meet at any of the usual spots."

"Got it, and Eternity is ready whenever you are," she said, leaving the room quickly. I turned my eyes back to the still-silent woman who was throwing daggers at me with her beautiful eyes.

"You know, you're even more sexy when you're angry."

"Flattery will get you absolutely nowhere, nigga. Don't get this pretty face fucked up, because I'm part Dominican."

I had to laugh at the sudden change to her speech and attitude. "What's the other part of that mixture?"

"Italian."

"Oh shit, now I know I'm not fucking with you or giving you a gun." I took a step back, still smiling.

"Devaughn. Dee. This shit is serious. The police are one thing, but people want you dead! Is that registering to you?"

"Someone's always wanted me dead for some reason of another, so yes, it's registered, but as fucked up as it seems, I'm use to it. What I need from you right now is just a little cooperation and for you to rest up so you can heal." I fluffed her pillows and gave her some more water. Standing over her, I was held captive by her remarkable beauty. Unable to help myself, I found my hand softly caressing her lovely cheek, wanting to kiss her, but not sure of her reaction. So much was going on and there was absolutely no time for romance. But what if I walked out that door and never came back? It was a moment born of mutual understanding of the uncertainty of the immediate future as I bent down and slowly touched my lips to hers. The taste of her was a mystery that sent my mind spinning in pace with the sensations she had shooting through my body when our tongues met for the first time. Deeper, I probed and searched her mouth, seeking to make love with just this part of our bodies. Though I wanted to take her forever, I backed away from her reluctantly. Relationships by nature were complicated. With her being my P.O., it made it worse because she could get into trouble for fuckin' with me.

"What was that for?"

"I'm not sure. It's gonna seem corny, but I couldn't see myself leaving without experiencing the pleasure of your magic. I knew to kiss you would be amazing, but damn, baby, you got a nigga ready to propose marriage."

That got a laugh from her, even though I could tell it hurt her a lot, too. "No need to take it that far. We haven't even agreed on a lunch date. Besides the conflict of you being alive long enough to date me, the fact remains I'm still your parole officer. I can't overlook that."

"I can keep a secret if you can. Besides, the best love stories are made when two people from different sides of the tracks hook up. That shit be explosive."

"True. But you are asking me to give up everything I know for you, and we just met. So let's take it slow and share a meal first."

"What's your favorite thing to eat?" I asked, making the sexual implication known.

"What's yours?" she countered, meeting the challenging look in my eyes.

"Pussy, but I haven't had the pleasure to taste that delicacy in a while."

"You could've fooled me with the way you had that young girl babbling earlier."

"I haven't ate her. I just utilized my other talents."

"Mm, really?"

"Maybe one day you'll know first-hand," I told her, walking toward the door."

"Dee?"

"Yeah?"

"Seventy-two hours, and then I take over without any questions."

"Anything else?" I asked, standing in the doorway.

"Yeah, stop smoking weed or I'ma give you a piss test!"

My laughter echoed down the hall, and I was still smiling while cutting across the grass to the house in the distance. I wasn't sure what was going on with me and Ramona, or even it there should be a me and her, but I knew that I liked her. It wasn't just her looks, although they were perfect. She had some swagger underneath that judicial system polish, and I liked that.

"Glad to see you're all smiles, considering your kids are in here worried sick," Mikko said, snatching the door open before I could knock.

"Damn, woman, you stay on my back. Shut the fuck up sometimes," I told her, pushing past her into the house, then going into the living room where my kids sat looking at the news.

"Hey, Dad," Day-Day said, getting up to give me a hug.

"Hey, sweetheart. What up, Lil' M and La-La?"

Deshana came over to hug me, too. Latavia just sat there, looking at me through bloodshot eyes that had seen too much.

"To prison, huh? Three days, Dad. That's gotta be some type of fucking record." Defeat laced her every word.

"Come on Latav—"

"No, fuck that, Deshana! You keep wanting to take up for him, but you saw the news like the rest of us. He killed that woman in broad daylight, and you think they not gonna lock his ass back up?"

"First of all, I didn't kill anybody, because she's very much alive. Secondly, didn't tell muthafuckas to start shooting at me when I came out of the courthouse, but it happened, and I dealt with it. One thing for goddamn sure, and that's that I ain't going back to prison, no matter what!"

"You know what you are? You're just a walking dead man who don't know it." She ran from the room.

"Latavia!" Day-Day yelled.

"Let her go, sweetheart." I sat on the couch. By now Mikko had come into the room, but she said nothing as she smoked her cigarette. I understood why my daughter was mad, but her words still stung badly.

"How much of what they say is true?" Deshana asked, she and Day-Day taking seats beside me.

"It's retaliation for the meeting. I just didn't expect it to come so soon or play out like it did. I think the other niggas who were there have been volunteering information, but I'll deal with that later."

"So, what's the plan?"

"Well, I gotta take a trip real quick and find that out. You coming?"

"Yeah, already knew that."

"Who—"

"Now hold it a damn minute. My daughter ain't going no-muthafuckin'-where with you right now, not with all this shit going on."

"Mom, I can take care of myself."

"You better shut you goddamn mouth before I shut it for you."

"Mikko, listen, whether you like it or not, our children are grown up. And as such, they can and will make their own decisions. She's safe with me, I promise you that."

"How can you make that promise when an innocent bystander got hit because of you yesterday?"

"Because I can and will die for any of my kids, and you know that."

Silence filled the room as the conversation between me and Mikko continued with our eyes. I'd given my life up once already in a way that was worse than anything, and based on that alone, she knew I spoke the truth.

"I love you Day-Day." I kissed her and stood up.

"I love you too, Daddy, just be safe out there."

I stepped right in front of my ex until we were eye-to-eye. The woman before me wasn't a stranger. She was simply made bitter by the hand life had dealt her, and I understood that better than most. Without caring, I cupped her face and kissed her with thirty-three years of love and hate, stealing her breath and replacing it with my own. Feeling the heat start at my toes and work its way up quickly, I kissed her harder, deeper, giving her all the passion I knew she still remembered from our past mixed with the fire of what may be done for our future. I felt her arms wrap themselves around me, pulling me to shore after a long time at sea, and I felt my hate close a little more. Pulling back, I stared down into her closed eyes as they fluttered open and looked back at me. She could see me, my lust and desire, and just beneath that the love that I use to know.

"Let's go, Lil' M." I released her from my grasp and walked quickly out the front door toward the main house.

"What was that about, Dad?"

"A reminder. She needed to remember the nigga I've always been in her life, because she never doubted me before."

"What do you think she's thinking now?"

"She's thinking about the last time we made love," I said with arrogance entwined in my smile.

"Do you remember?"

"Like it was yesterday."

"So, what's next?"

"We've got a meeting with the soldiers. Whether it's convenient or not, it's a war going on, and I damn sure plan to win." I knew it was premature to give the orders I was planning to issue without first consulting those in the chain of command, but I didn't need my hand held right now. Undoubtedly I was already in hot water, so it was better for me to make these moves now while I still had the authority to do so.

"Everyone's in the gym," Keyz said when we came through the door. We made the quick trip down in the elevator, and the doors opened on a massive crowd quietly talking amongst themselves.

"You ready?" I asked her under my breath.

"I was made for this, Pops."

And with that, we stepped onto the basketball court. Immediately all conversations ceased, and every pair of eyes landed on me. I took a moment to evaluate these men and women before me, the set lines of determination creasing the faces of most, and some looks of terror on others. I didn't know these people, but I felt a loyalty and responsibility for their lives because they'd pledged their life to the same cause I had all those years ago. Most people thought being a part of a gang or an organization was for the weak-minded or those who couldn't stand alone. Nobody really stopped to think how hard it was to stand for a set of beliefs that a lot didn't fully understand because they condemned it without researching it. They thought it was a joke, a game, or just a passing trend. I wasn't above enlightenment, and the first thing I wanted to be known was that no one can appreciate peace without war. The situation may have seemed overly dramatic because it all stood behind a single question. It wasn't the question — it was the disrespect.

"Peace, Blood!"

"Peace, Almighty!"

"By now you've all heard what's going on, but you may not know why it's going on. At the very least, I owe you an explanation."

I proceeded to run down the meeting that took place, not leaving out any word spoken or action carried out. I delivered this speech without any emotion, closely watching the actions of those before me to see if they understood the price they had to be willing to pay for respect. I needed them to believe it wasn't just about me, because I was my brother's keeper. He was me, and I was him, so all of us had to have the same beliefs about how important it was to be respected at all costs.

"This is how it's going down: we've got to hit back, and hit hard. Anything that has to do with them is a target, and I want it eliminated without hesitation. Keep in mind that them peoples is watching, and move accordingly. We're not just out to kill everybody, we're taking over territory too, and anybody who questions it with the slightest hint of aggression will be dealt with. Remember to follow the chain of command at all times, and I want a report every forty-eight hours from the superiors. If it ain't broke, don't fix it!"

"It's EMU, bitch!" everyone chanted back.

With that, I left Keyz to deal with the individual assignments while I pulled Candy and Deshana to the side.

"Listen, I don't know how good or bad this meeting could go in a few hours, but if it starts to feel bad at all, you know how we're gonna handle it."

"But Dad, if you carry it like that, you're signing your own death certificate."

"Baby, if shit crazy, that means they were planning to kill me anyway." I smiled at her despite the harsh reality we were talking about. "In the mean time, I want you both to get everything you need, because as soon as it gets good and dark, we're on the move."

"Got it, Dad," she said, leaving.

"Can I speak to you for a moment in private?" Candy asked, scanning the room to see who was paying attention. I nodded my head and led her to the waiting elevator. We made the ride up in silence, but instead of going to the main floor, she pushed the button for the library. The doors opened onto what easily had to be thousands of books lining the walls of a two-story room with a cathedral-like arching ceiling. I'd never seen so many books in one place, and I scarcely had time to now with the speed in which I was being led across the floor to a door at the far end of the library. When the door opened, we stepped into a room about half the size of the first, with books along its walls, too, and two comfortable-looking leather recliners in the corner.

"Is all this necessary?"

"Just listen to me for a second, and don't say anything until I'm done."

"Go ahead, Candy." I sat down patiently.

"Look, we told Keyz that we wouldn't fuck no more, but—Fuck it! I love you, okay? And I'm starting to fall for you, but before you say anything about how impossible that is and how fucked up the timing is, all I'm saying is I know we can't be together, but we can at least have one more time."

I'd have been lying if I said I was shocked. I'd have been an even bigger liar if I said I didn't want her, too. I just didn't have time to complicate my life any more than it already was. I stood up and looked down into her tantalizing hazel eyes that shone back at me with complete submission and vulnerability, knowing I shouldn't say yes, but I couldn't say no. Slowly, while still looking at her, I began to undress. Taking off each piece of clothing, I watched her surveying my body with an intensity that gave me chills in the best possible way.

"Your turn," I whispered once I stood before her completely naked. Looking on with the same mesmerized intensity, I admired the luscious curves of her body when she eased her jeans and panties down to her feet, kicking them and her shoes off. Quickly following that came her wife-beater, under which she wore her bra to hold the firm, yet succulent breasts that I was slowly caressing. Pulling her to me, I let one hand fall between her legs, my finger started to dance into her sea of sweet moisture, catching her purr of pleasure when I captured her waiting lips with my own. Her body's response was immediate, as was my own, causing me to push further inside her when she grabbed my dick as if it was hers to have indefinitely. If this was to be our last time, then I didn't just want to fuck or simply have sex — I wanted to make love to her.

Gently, I lowered her body to the soft, shaggy carpet, never breaking the rhythm of the dance our mouths were crooning to, still swirling slow circles inside her. I could feel the temperature in her body rising, demanding more and making sure the last peaks of blissful satisfaction could be seen from the valleys below. Finally breaking the spell our lips had been under, I pulled back so I could gaze upon her full beauty. Her eyes had glazed over with need, and I knew mine spoke the same message. Removing my fingers, I held them up for her to see her glistening juices before I stuck them in my mouth, savoring the flavor of her. Starting with her neck, I set forth on the task to kiss, lick, and suck every inch of her body. Not neglecting my part, I travelled all the way to her toes and back up to her sweet spot. Without pause, I submerged my tongue inside her, exploring and enjoying the flavors of her almost as much as her pants and pleas. With no mercy, my tongue danced with her clit, sending her over the edge, causing systematic tremors to rock her body while my name escaped her mouth in a strangled scream. Taking all she had to offer, I tortured her still. As I put my dick at her pussy lips, it parted her welcoming safe haven inch by inch until I felt the storm rebuild inside her.

"Dee, please," she whimpered, tears leaking out the corners of her eyes.

"Shhh, I got you, baby. Hold onto me." And with that, the rhythm began of slow, yet thorough strokes with me pulling almost completely out of her, only to slide back like a well-oiled piston.

"I can't, Dee. I can't. You have to— Mm, please, baby."

No response was needed, because I felt the beast break his leash, causing me to pummel her faster and harder.

"Oh God! Dee, I'm. I'm. Shit, I love you."

Faster still, I gave her my good loving, feeling her rising to the challenge and raising her hips to meet me when she enveloped me with her legs.

"Look at me," I demanded huskily, pounding into her until I felt the earth shake and I came as hard as I had in my dream.

I didn't try to move, did nothing except look down at the woman beneath me, who was crying silent tears. Her eyes said so much, held so many promises, but I didn't feel like I deserved half of them. Kissing her softly, I rolled onto my side and pulled her still-shaking naked body to mine.

"Why are you crying, babe?"

"I don't know. What we did, what just happened was beautiful. We touched. No, you touched something inside me that no one will ever be able to replace. It's bittersweet. This is a bittersweet moment, and I never fully understood what that meant until now."

"It doesn't have to be over, it's just crazy right now. And I'm not sure of exactly what I feel, but I know I'm feeling you a lot. It's more than sex, more than lust, I just don't know if I'm ready or deserving of it yet."

"Baby, you deserve to be happy." She cupped my face with her trembling hands.

"Time is all I'm asking, sweetheart."

"And time is the one thing we don't have," she whispered kissing me with a passion and tenderness that set my body ablaze again with need. The realization that I wasn't just wanting Candy, but starting to need her, made me pull back as thoughts of my sister filled my mind. The last thing I wanted to do was hurt her. Pulling her to her feet. We dressed in silence and retraced our steps onto the elevator, taking it to the main floor.

As soon as the doors opened, Keyz was right there, suspicion masking her whole face.

"Where the fuck y'all been?"

"First of all, we ain't been together the whole time, and even if we were, I told you what the fuck we was doing, so what's the problem?"

"Why are her nipples hard, Dee?" she asked, spitting venom in Candy's direction. I turned to look at Candy's chest, and she didn't try to shield my view, but smiled instead.

"I hadn't noticed, but thanks for pointing that out, sis," I replied, reaching like I intended to lift up the wife beater to get a better look at the chest I could still see heaving beneath me in pleasure.

"Uh, muthafucka, back up." The tension relaxed from her face a little at a time.

"For real, what's up, sis?"

"Shit, I just wanted to see you before you left."

"Yeah, we about to do that now, I was just getting Candy to make sure we have everything we need in the truck for the trip." Taking my hint, Candy started to head outside, but Keyz caught her hand and pulled her into a powerful kiss that left me scratching my chin. I hoped like hell she couldn't smell the scent of our love making on her, and luckily Candy had the good sense to make it a good kiss and a better performance of reluctantly having to part ways.

"You trying to make me jealous?"

She laughed at that, but there was something in her eyes that said it seemed false.

"Alright, I gotta go," she put her arms around me and kissed me, catching my bottom lip in between both of hers and sucking on it slightly before I jerked back.

"Kiara, what the—"

"It's funny. You taste like Candy." She spun on her heel and disappeared under the staircase. Sighing heavily, I walked outside and hopped in the waiting truck.

"Let's go." Taking the blunt Deshana offered me, I smoked in a brooding silence while my mind traveled back and forth between Candy, Keyz, and my meeting. I had too much going on, and I couldn't run the risk of alienating my sister. No matter how much I felt for her girl at the moment, I was just gonna have to steer clear of Candy, and my mind turned over to a welcome distraction in the form of a half-Italian, half-Dominican bombshell lying in my bed. There were possibilities there, and it was a lot safer than Candy right now.

"You alright, Dad? You're quiet as shit over there."

"Yeah, I'm good, I just got a lot on my mind."

"What did she say when I left, Dee?"

"She kissed me."

"Okay, what was that supposed to mean?"

"No, when I say she kissed me, I ain't talking about a peck. She caught my bottom lip in between hers and started to suck on it."

"*What*?" Both women yelled in unison.

"That wasn't the bad part. When I pulled back and asked what the fuck was going on, she says it's funny that I taste like you, and walked off."

"But why would you taste like her? Wow, bitch ,is you fucking my aunt and my father?" Deshana asked hostilely, looking like she was ready to start swinging.

"Lil' M, that ain't none of your muthafuckin' business, so don't get too grown."

"Come on, Dad, that's some straight bullshit, and you know it. What you should do is make up with mom so she'll stop being so damn mean, because you know you love her as much as she does you."

"What, you cupid now?"

"Nah, but I'm saying you fucking with this bitch, and—"

"You got one more time to call me bitch. That's it, girl, and sure is gonna get real ugly in minute, muthafucka."

"Ah, both of y'all chill the fuck out."

Nobody said anything, but they threw daggers at each other for the better part of an hour while I smoked cigarette after cigarette to calm my nerves. A couple of times I caught Eternity smirking at me in the rear mirror, and once she was even licking her lips at me. I needed more pussy problems like I needed a hole in my head.

"Deshana, I love your aunt, and we've been together for a long time now, but I love your father, too."

"How do you love him when you've only known him a whole week?"

"Keyz told me everything about him from the time we first got together. She even let me read his entry and talk to him on the phone, and then when he came home, she told me she didn't want him fucking with just any bitch, so she chose me, and now Now I'm falling in love with a man for only the second time in my life. And I'm scared as shit. I don't want to hurt Keyz or your father, but I don't know how not to love them both."

Again, nobody said anything as we ate up the distance on the highway with everyone traveling in their own respective thoughts.

"Eternity, where are we?"

"Just entering Norfolk."

I picked up the cellphone and dialed a number from memory. The phone was picked up immediately.

"Where are you?"

"Just got to the hospital. Where do you wanna meet?"

"We can meet in public if you'd like. How about NSU campus?"

"I'll be there in a minute." I disconnected.

"Eternity, Norfolk State University campus."

"Why there, Dad?"

"I don't know, but it's out in the open, which means public. When we get out, Candy, you're gonna step out with me. Lil' M, you bring up the rear. And Eternity, you stay in the truck with the baby Uzi locked, cocked, and ready to rock if I give the signal." I hit the button for the gun compartment, grabbing glocks and the Uzi. I passed the Uzi up front and handing Candy one of the glocks. The other one went in the small of my back, but the extended clip made it feel awkward and hard to conceal.

"Look, Candy. I'm sorry I called you a bitch. I get that you love them both, and I feel for you being stuck in that situation. All I can say it that I hope you know what you're doing. You too, Dad."

"Yeah, yeah, just stay focused, because we're pulling up."

"Thanks, Deshana." Candy held her gun out so they could touch glocks.

I saw him standing next to an all-black Expedition, flanked on both sides by a five-man team. As soon as we came to a stop, I opened the door and hopped out, Candy and Deshana right behind me.

"What's poppin', big homie?" I offered him my hand to throw up our hood with and giving him a hug.

"Y'all know what it is, my nigga. You, and me, this movement."

"More so, look, I know shit looks crazy right now, but I got everything under control."

"Who those bitches in the middle of Blood business?" he asked, gesturing toward the two women behind me. The way the question was asked put all the soldiers out here on alert, eyes shifting, hands getting itchy.

"Come on, my nigga, I know you remember Lil' M from when she use to come visit me?"

"Damn, my fault, fool. What's poppin', lil' mama?"

"Dat Almighty."

"Okay, okay, I smell that. So, who's this other sexy-ass bitch?" I felt my teeth grind involuntarily. The way he kept calling them bitches was starting to bother me, but I kept my cool.

"This my new recruit." I stood quiet while he appraised her, but it wasn't blood lust I saw in his eyes, it was just lust.

"So, you got everything under control?"

"No doubt."

"Then why the fuck is your face on every news station between here and Colorado? And please tell me why the fuck you murdered five Shine niggas without my consent!"

"The nigga Bezo disrespected me, and G-Mack let that shit slide. I couldn't let it slide, so I—"

"Nigga, we got one more time. To say 'I like you' ain't part of an organization," he intoned in a menacing whisper. This time hands went instantly to pockets and behind backs, and I could feel Candy and Deshana tensing up behind me. I was just hoping that one of them didn't move prematurely.

"My bad, homie."

"What's the situation with the police?"

"My P.O. is taking care of that, so they won't lock me up for the shooting in front of the courthouse."

"And what's this shit about shells matching a shooting in a residential neighborhood right by your babies' mama's house?"

"Some niggas followed me from the pen."

"Why did you still have the same gun?"

"I don't have an answer for that." It was stupid of me not to get rid of the gun, but the unbelievable part of it all was that the exact same gun was in the truck right now.

"No answer for that, huh?"

"No."

"Good, because I detest hearing bullshit come from your mouth. You've disappointed me greatly, Devaughn. You've been home two days, and already you front page news. Where I come from, that's called a liability. I don't want you to retaliate against Shine. I'm gonna handle that situation for you. What I want you to do is go underground and wait until I tell you it's safe to come out. Do you understand?"

"Yeah."

"Alright then." And with that, he turned to the door already being held open by one of his men.

Deshana opened my door and Candy climbed in before me. That's when I heard it. They didn't come speeding up like they had before. No, this time they came creeping. Instinct made me reach for my gun, but it was too late.

"Shine up!"

The impact of the first bullet pushed me back, and the second one spun me around and threw me against the black expedition that was there and then gone. I could hear the sound of the baby Uzi dumping shells a mile a minute, but it seemed far off in the distance. Somebody screamed, and then I was looking up into the face of Candy. She was cradling my head in her lap, but steadily pumping bullets at a target I couldn't see. Everything seemed so far away, and the warm summer evening had turned unbearably cold.

"Hold on, Dee. Come on, baby, hold on," Candy cried over and over. I felt her tears hit my face as the night closed in around us, and I felt nothing when the blackness swallowed me whole.

Chapter 7

Who Can You Trust?

"A lot of blood."

"Operate."

"Unlikely."

"Heart."

I could only catch pieces of conversation that were trying to register in my mind, but the immense pain I was in was making it hard to clear a path for thinking. It really wasn't hard to figure out how serious it was, because the look on the tear-stained face hovering in the background said it all. This time I didn't fight when unconsciousness sucked me down the rabbit hole again.

When I came back around, the steady beeping told me where I was which, considering that I woke up at all, wasn't an entirely bad thing. But when my hand movement was immediately restricted by the handcuff attached to my bed, I knew I was fucked for real. I didn't want to open my eyes, didn't want to face the harsh reality after years of waiting on freedom. I was right back where I started. I felt the weight of depression hit me like a ton.

Thoughts of escape flooded my mind. I couldn't go back to prison, I wouldn't, so I had to find some way to get the hell out. And go where? Memories of what happened and how I ended up here came crashing in on my still-reeling mind, forcing me to ask myself who was still on my team, or did I even have a team to play for? There's no such thing as coincidence, meaning them nigga's crew knew where I was gonna be probably before I did. The pain of my gunshot wounds was coming back with an intense throb, but the pain of betrayal hurt so much more than anything physical ever would. I wasn't in the frame of mind to analyze, and I let the constantly-building hatred wrap itself around me like a mother's love to her newborn.

I wasn't a religious person, but I believed in God. In the last twenty years, I'd only had cause to say one prayer, and it raced from my mouth now.

"God, protect me from my friends and the hand of my enemies."

"Daddy!" Deshana cried, causing me to snap my eyes open and see her bolt from the chair she'd been resting in at my bedside.

"Hey, Lil' M," I whispered, clearing my throat and sending pain shooting through my body.

"Oh, Daddy."

"Shh, don't cry, baby girl, I'm okay. It hurts like hell, but I'm guessing I'll live. Now, where are the police?"

"Outside. There's two of them. You're in a hospital in Norfolk. Dad, I'm so sorry, but we had to bring you to the hospital. You were bleeding so much, and you were unconscious, and—"

"It's alright, I'm not mad. I know you all were just trying to save my life. That's more than I can say for some. Where's Candy and Eternity?"

"They've both been at a safe house close by since the— Well, since we brought you here. Keyz was here yesterday, but she went back home when she got a mysterious call. I talked to her two hours ago, and she's on her way back now."

"Yesterday? Shit, how long have I been out?"

"It's been three days. The bullet in your chest grazed your heart, so they had to crack you open and operate. The second one went straight through your shoulder, but it was a fucking .44 slug, and it tore you up pretty bad. I'm just so glad you're awake." She took my hand and squeezed it.

"Where are your mom, sisters and brother?"

"I didn't. I didn't tell them. I knew if they found out they would come down here, and that's too many targets when we can't separate friend from foe. The only reason Keyz let me stay is because of this." She held up the glock. "I told her I'd shoot her if she tried to make me leave."

I had to smile at that, especially since I could imagine the look on my sister's face.

"Put that away. So, what have the cops said?"

"They wanna know who shot you, but mainly they wanna know where you P.O.'s body is."

"Yes, Mr. Mitchell, where is Mrs. Petra's body?" asked a plain-clothed detective with a badge swinging from his neck. I stared blankly at him and the cop that came in the door behind him, the stink of authority leaving an all-too-familiar bad taste in my mouth.

"Her body is where it's at, officers."

"And where might it be at, Mr. Mitchell? But before you answer that, let me read you your rights."

"That's okay, I know my rights."

The officer ignored my response and went on with his duty of reading me my rights. When he was done, he said, "Alright, so where's it at?"

"Where it is."

At first neither got what I was saying, but it didn't take long for him to realize what was going on.

"That's fine, smartass, but you're still gonna burn for it." Heated anger created beads of sweat on his forehead.

Or was it something more? Suddenly shit didn't feel right, and it wasn't just the ordinary feelings I'd had when facing cops handcuffed. So far, the other cop hadn't said anything, but I could tell he was uneasy, and that didn't make sense considering he had the upper hand in a major way. Looking at my daughter, I could tell she sensed what I was feeling, and I could see her hands shift slightly beneath the blanket sitting in her lap.

"Officers I'm gonna have to insist that you talk to my lawyer if you have questions, but in the meantime, I suggest you un-cuff me."

"Oh, silly me." The detective slapped his head with the heel of his hand. "I forgot to tell you that the Fairfax court has requested that you be detained until you can be properly questioned about certain activities in their jurisdiction. So I'll kindly have to ask you to shut the fuck up and stick around." A malicious grin spread across his face.

"You can't talk to—"

At that moment the door opened again, and as if on cue, in came my little sister and a few guests I was relieved to see.

"Gentlemen, I'll have to ask — better yet, demand — that you un-cuff and step away from my client immediately," my attorney said, smiling at the rapidly-changing faces of the cops.

"This man is wanted in connection with a kidnapping and murder of a government employee in another jurisdiction, and we've been instructed to hold him until such time as he's able to travel back to the county of origin."

"The murder and kidnapping of whom, may I ask?"

"Of his probation officer, one Mrs. Ramona Petras, or haven't you been watching the news?"

At this question, Dale grinned at the detective. I'd seen that smile before — it was one of secret victory right before the curtain came up on the final act.

And then it happened. Stepping aside, my lawyer allowed my second guest to step forward, although she was moving awkwardly because she was still in pain.

"For your information, it's Ms. Petras, and I'll ask you kindly not to fuck up my name." An innocent smile graced her face, bringing much-needed light to my day. The way the cops' eyes popped out of their heads would have been appropriate if they had seen a ghost or Halley Berry naked.

"Wha-what's this? You're dead. I mean, everyone thought you were dead."

"Well, as you can see, I'm alive and, well, shot, I'm still good, and like Mr. Race just said, you need to un-cuff Mr. Mitchell now!"

I couldn't be sure which temperament was more volatile, the Italian side or the Dominican, but from the looks of it, she was about to give it with both barrels. The silence reached for a long thirty seconds before my bracelet was removed and the cops hauled ass out of the room.

"Nice going, Ms. Petras, but what the hell are you doing out of bed?" I asked, projecting as much bass and authority as I could.

"It's been seventy-two hours, Mr. Mitchell, plus you went and got your dumb-ass shot."

I could see the anger in her eyes, but it was masking something that I couldn't quite make out. Either way, I was glad the cavalry came before my daughter was wanted for two counts of capital murder.

"Thanks." I squeezed her hand when she slumped into the chair next to my bed.

"Yeah, yeah. We're even. So what the fuck happened, Dee?"

"Uh, I'm gonna have to advise my client not to answer that question until after we've had time to confer."

She didn't pay any attention to him, just continued to look at me expectantly. Winking at her and squeezing her hand again, I turned to my sister, who'd been entirely too quiet.

"Keyz?"

"I'm okay. I'm holding it together. How are you feeling?"

"Like I've been shot, bitch." I smiled despite the pain.

"I've talked to the doctor, and he gave me the prescriptions for your medication. The paperwork is already done, so all we gotta do is get you dressed and we can get the hell out of here."

"Candy and Eternity?"

"Outside in the truck. And a few friends."

"A few? Shit, it's like the fucking USMC out there, muthafucka," Ramona said, chuckling with felt humor.

"Are you sure they're friends?" Deshana asked.

"Yes, I'm sure. What do you say, Big Head, you ready to go?"

"Any word of him?"

"Not now, Dee," she replied, casting a not-so-subtle glance at Ramona.

"Dale, what am I looking at?"

"Absolutely nothing for now. Ms. Petras made sure you're in the clear about everything involving that incident. As for Norfolk, well, you were simply the victim of a senseless crime. They haven't asked that once you leave, you don't come back."

"Who's got my clothes?"

"Right here." Keyz held up a bag and pulled out black sweatpants, a black t-shirt, brand new all-black Air Force Ones, and a black hoody.

"Oh yeah?" I asked, looking deep into her eyes and finding the message: *It's time to go old school.*

I remembered telling her that, once upon a time, it didn't matter if someone saw me at 7:00 a.m. or p.m., they could always find me wearing black sweats, a black hoody, a black T-shirt, black shoes, and a black pistol with black thoughts of doing some ill shit as soon as the opportunity presented itself. It was time now to get back on my bullshit, when it was just me and mine fighting for everything we got.

"Well, who's got the honor of dressing me?" I'd asked this question looking directly at Ramona, but all she did was smile and shake her head.

"I got it, everybody clear out. Deshana, tell everybody to be ready, because we'll be out in a minute. And tell my girl to get in my car. Ms. Petras, you can ride back with Dee."

As quietly as they'd came, everyone left the room until it was just me and Keyz.

She said nothing for a minute and simply stared at me, leaving it up to me to decipher what was running through her mind. I could tell she'd spent a lot of time crying in the last few days because of the redness surrounding her eyes with the slight swelling, but I didn't see tears in her eyes now. What I saw was determination and hunger. I'd given her the path on this way of life for the most part, but this dose of reality had put a slight madness in the shine of her eyes. I could tell something had broken, but this time I didn't know if even I could fix it.

"You okay?"

"I should be asking you that question, since you're the one that just had a face-to-face with death."

"I'm alright. Besides, I knew the rules of the game being played."

"The rules? The rules? Nigga, the fucking rules say loyalty is not an option! You were right to kill them disrespectful-ass niggas, and if you hadn't, I would've. But even if it was wrong, that still doesn't justify this!" she yelled, gesturing toward me lying in a hospital bed for emphasis.

I'd made a big miscalculation with my observations. I'd never seen a rage in her like a storm she was begging to unleash on something or someone. I now understood plainly what had broken inside her — her belief.

"Kiara, I love you more than all the words in the books in the world. Dead or alive, nothing will ever change that, so listen to what I'm about to say even if you don't want to hear it. I'm not a part of an organization, this organization, for just the niggas. Purpose is the purpose on which we founded it, because I believe in that, and I believe in those who had the balls to create the movement. I don't want you to lose faith in that or why we do what we do, okay?"

Her tears were back, but I couldn't tell if it was anger or pain that brought them. Seeing them still caused me pain.

"Dee, all I care about is you. You are what I believe in, what I would willingly give my life for, so know and understand that no matter who everybody was, anyone having part of you getting shot has to die. Everyone." The passion with which she spoke told me how serious she was, and that now it wasn't just a war we were fighting. It was payback.

"Come on, let's get me dressed so we can disappear."

The task was completed in silence, and then she helped me into a wheelchair for my ride through the narrow and somewhat deserted halls. Up until that point, I'd never realized it was obviously the middle of the night, but it didn't matter to me, because I wanted to be anywhere but in some hospital. When we got out front, I saw what Ramona had meant by an army, because despite the early morning hour, that parking lot was full of soldiers standing next to their rides, on the lookout for anything posing a threat. My truck was parked directly in front of the entrance, and when we came out, Deshana opened the door.

"I can walk from here." I rose slowly and adjusted the sling on my injured arm. It felt like I still had hot lead in my chest, but I didn't, care because the pain reminded me I was alive.

"I'm so glad you're okay," Candy said, running up and wrapping her arms around me gently.

"You ladies took care of me and handled business. Thank you for that."

"Oh, Dee. I was so scared."

"There will be time," I whispered to her, releasing her so I could be helped into the back of the truck. Everyone loaded up, and a forty-car motorcade left the seven cities of VA behind at a quick pace. Deshana and Ramona were riding with me, but no one was in the mood for conversation. Every one of us understood the stakes of the game had been raised, and there was no second place. It was all for keeps.

"Roll up," I told Deshana, opening the armrest and tossed her everything she needed. Unsurprisingly, she didn't even flinch at the fact that my P.O. was in the ride with us.

"Are you really gonna smoke a blunt in front of me?" she asked, attitude and disbelief running a relay race with her words.

"No, I'm probably gonna smoke a few."

"Do you think I won't violate your black ass or something? I've got a good mind to do it just so you won't get shot, or worse, shoot somebody."

"Trust me, Ramona, at this point if it wasn't a gun, it'd be a knife."

That comment shut her up as the full weight of what was going on came hurdling toward her. I'd been out six days, been in three gunfights, and managed to get both of us shot. This was in no way a game. Shit was almost bad enough to be a really good movie.

Deshana rolled the blunt and passed it to me. I wanted to hit it as hard as I could, but my chest still hurt like a sumabitch, so I had to slow roll with it. To her credit, she didn't say anything at first, but somehow I knew that wasn't gonna last. When she did speak, it fucked me up, though, and made me cough until I felt like my chest would rip open.

"Pass that shit to me, damn!"

"Oh my God, Dad, are you okay?"

"I'm good. I'm good. Uh, what did you say, Ms. Petras?"

"I said stop trying to smoke all the damn weed and pass the blunt, nigga."

Dumbfounded, I did like I was told. She looked like she was gonna hit it cautiously, which would've been a good idea, but somehow between point A and point B her pride got in the way, and she hit that muthafucka like she ain't missed a day smoking in fifteen years. I laughed until tears rolled down my face when she started coughing and choking until her pretty little face turned bright red. I knew it was wrong to laugh at her, but she brought the shit on herself.

"Goddamn, what the fuck is this?" she asked, staring with an angry fascination at the still-smoldering marijuana in her hand.

"That, my sweet Ramona, is black diamond, one of the most powerful hybrids of weed grown today."

"Where did you...? Never mind, dumb question. Shit, one hit and I'm already on the moon." That didn't stop her from hitting it two more times, using extreme caution, before sending it to Deshana.

I could tell by her expression that she didn't agree with getting high with what she perceived to be the enemy, but it was my show. She shrugged as if to say fuck it. Me, on the other hand — shit, I was more curious than ever about this mystery lady riding beside me.

"Where are you from, Ramona?" I asked, getting the blunt back.

"Originally from New York. Hell's Kitchen, to be exact, but I moved to Baltimore when I was eight years old."

"So that's why you don't have the accent. Do you ever go home to visit?"

"All the time, and its only certain times that my accent comes out, but that generally means I'm probably cussing you out in another language."

I passed her the blunt back. "How many languages do you speak?"

"A few, why?"

"I think it's sexy when a woman can speak different languages. I don't care if she's cussing me out, that shit still sounds sexy."

"Well, my favorite is the language of love. Everything sounds so sensual."

"You mean French?"

"No, fool, Spanish." She laughed and handed the blunt to Deshana, who seemed to be trapped in her own thoughts.

"I took Spanish three times in high school and failed every damn time! I just couldn't get it, and by the time I figured out I would've gotten so many more girls if I'd known it, it was too late."

"So wait, you never dated a Latina?"

"I didn't say that, I just said I didn't know Spanish."

"Oh, excuse me, big playa."

"I know you ain't talking with the way you look. You probably had more niggas running around than the athletics department as a whole."

"Did you just call me a ho?"

"See, that's— That's bullshit, because I didn't say you was fucking everybody."

"Don't get fucked up, Dee."

"Promise?" I asked, flashing her my biggest seductive smile. Out of the corner of my eye, I could tell Deshana was staring a hole through the side of my head, so I steered the conversation back toward safer ground.

In the end, we dropped the T.V. down so we could watch the basketball game and smoked another blunt. By the time we pulled up to the house, everybody was high as a muthafucka and starting to doze off. I knew before I could get any real sleep that I would need another installment of my wonderful pain medication. Stepping out of the truck, the sun was just rising, and for the moment I had to stand there and bask in nature's beauty. It was never far from my mind that I almost didn't get to enjoy this shit again, and suddenly I felt a reinforced motivation to neutralize and eliminate all my frenemies.

"Let everybody know that there's a meeting at 3:00 p.m., only the top people," I told Keyz when she walked over to me.

"Done."

"Where are you putting all these soldiers?"

"They're going back to Tidewater to see what they can find out, or until we call."

"We're safe here, this is our territory."

"I hope you're right. Deshana, go get some sleep, baby. I'm fine now. Come see me whenever after you sleep, but not before 2:00 p.m."

"Okay, Daddy," she replied, giving me a hug and starting off across the grass.

"Eternity?"

"Yes?" she answered, coming around the truck to stand in front of me.

"You did a good job. I don't remember a lot, but I remember hearing that Uzi singing to them niggas, and I want you to know that I appreciate that." I could see the tears welling in her eyes, and I pulled her toward me into a somewhat-clumsy embrace. "When I'm healed up, I owe you," I whispered in her ear, causing her to blush.

"Alright, Keyz, me and Ramona need our dope so we can fall into a nice coma and rest for a while."

With difficulty, we made it into the house and upstairs, where Ramona and I fell into the bed fully clothed.

"I'd love to take advantage of you right now, but I'm kinda handicapped," I told her, sleep coming almost instantly, but not before I heard her slurred and drowsy response.

"There'll be other times."

And at that, we both fell off the face of the earth.

My dreams were nightmares that mixed past with future. I saw a lot of people I'd murdered, people that would've murdered me if I hadn't trusted my instincts. I saw myself being tortured by my superiors, stabbed and shot, and then left for dead. The worst of it was when flashes of my daughters being tortured and raped entered the scenes. The pain of that was so horrifying it snapped me out of my sleep, drenched in sweat and breathing so hard I could hear my heart beating in my ears. It took me a few minutes to realize the things I'd seen weren't real, and the pain I was feeling was from being shot.

Slowly my breathing returned to normal, and I was able to hear soft, deep breathing of the beautiful woman lying next to me. Sometime during our sleep our hands had come together, and they stayed that way even now. Looking at her brought the beginnings of calm to my scattered thoughts, and that bought a tiny smile to my lips that matched hers. Even in her sleep, she smiled while she got the much-needed rest her body demanded. I could tell this woman was full of surprises, mysteries, and capable of incredible passion if she would let herself go there. Hopefully I could be the one to get her to open up so the world could see the beautiful flower inside of this gorgeous woman. Probably wishful thinking at best, considering the long road in front of me. I couldn't put her back in jeopardy of becoming an innocent victim, because next time that bullet could be her last.

A look at my watch on the nightstand showed it was a little after 1:00 p.m. I needed to get up, take a bath, and get my shit together for the meeting I'd called. Trying not to wake her, I slid silently from the bed, but when I tried to unlock our fingers, I met immediate resistance.

"Where are you going?"

"To take a bath. It's okay, I'm not leaving you."

"Why is it so dark in here? The house is clearly made of glass."

"Keyz closed the dome over the roof so no one could see in. Safety precaution. Why? I know you ain't scared of the dark."

"Shit, nigga, as dark as you are?" she replied, laughing and rubbing the sleep from her eyes.

"Fuck you, this complexion of black is called sexual chocolate. Sorry, we can't all have the golden, flawless skin with movie-star looks."

"I never said it wasn't sexy."

My look should have told her to keep it up and I'd open both of our gunshot wounds fucking the shit out of her.

"It's strange. I feel like I've known you forever. I know that sounds corny, but I've never been this forward with a guy I just met. I'm not saying I'm shy, but whatever is going on between us is happening unbelievably fast. I know with everything going on, commitment is the last thing on your mind, not to mention the other women who are madly in love with you. I'm not expecting anything from you, Dee. I just want you to know that despite everything, I still think you're one of the good guys. Hopefully you stay alive long enough for me to find out."

I could tell she was genuine about what she said and didn't say. More importantly, what I was starting to feel for her was different than what I felt for Candy, only I couldn't tell how just yet.

"I'm not going anywhere without a fight. Except to the tub." I walked into the closet and grabbed two towels and washcloths. When I came back out, she was still lying on the bed, staring at the ceiling, but I could tell she wasn't asleep.

"Come on." I took her hand and pulled her gently from the bed.

"But we can't. We're both fucked up!"

"I know, we're just gonna take a nice, relaxing bath in the Jacuzzi. Trust me, I won't hurt you."

"Yeah, now you say that, after one bullet played pinball with my vital organs," she replied, allowing me to lead her into the bathroom. "I don't have any clothes."

"Come on, all these women in this house and you think I can't get you something to wear? I think you'll look delicious in skin-tight Gucci jeans. Matter fact, hold on. Intercom on. Page Kiara to north wing master suit."

"Who the hell are you talking—" Before she could finish, the loudspeaker came on and the message was broadcasted.

"Damn, this house is something else. At least now I know how to track down your ass when you pull a disappearing act."

"So possessive already? I like that."

"Nah, nigga, it's just that every time you go out, shit always happens."

"What's up, Big Head? Everything alright?" Keyz asked, breezing into the room like a model fresh off the runway.

"Damn, you got a date or something?" I asked, admiring everything from the all-white, form-fitting dress that stopped at mid-thigh, to the five-inch, open-toed, all-white Manolo Blahnik's. Sometimes I forgot how beautiful she was when she got all dressed up. Flawless makeup, vicious hairdo. Shit, she belonged on the cover of a magazine, not in a pile of bodies surrounding me.

"No, I had a business meeting about the hotel expansion to Canada. Gotta keep the money flowing, ya dig?"

"Yeah, I dig, but listen, Ramona needs a wardrobe, so—"

"I don't need a new wardrobe, I just need something to wear."

"Sizes?"

"I wear a two, 36C cup, and size four shoe."

"Make sure to get her some thongs, too."

"Dee!"

"What, you need underwear too, right?"

"You're so embarrassing."

"Anyway, get the whole wardrobe, K. Take the money out of the safe if you need to."

"I got it, Dee. I'ma send somebody shopping right now. I'll see y'all later." She left the room, not covering that mischievous smile of her.

"Dee, I don't need you buying me a wardrobe. I've got plenty of clothes at my house."

"Will you please just chill out and let me do this? I got you, damn." Turning my attention back to the task at hand, I filled the tub up and turned the bubbles on. When I turned back to face her, she was throwing glaciers at me with her eyes.

"What?"

"I'm not for sale, Devaughn."

"I never thought you were, Ramona. Where did that come from?"

"You just told your sister to spend an obscene amount of money on me, and you don't even know me! Niggas just don't do that."

It was a battle for me to keep my temper in check, so I took a few moments to gather my thoughts before I spoke again.

"Sweetheart, I'm not trying to buy you, and you don't owe me shit. I'm only doing what any real nigga would do, and that's take care of you and treat you like the queen you are. I'm probably one of the few niggas who knows a woman's worth and that she's always the power behind the throne. Being that I know this and I like you, wouldn't it only be right that I treat you accordingly?"

I could tell she was weighing my words carefully. Obviously she came across her fair share of slick-talking muthafuckas who only wanted one thing. To say more would only put more mistrust in her sparkling black eyes, so I held my tongue and went about undressing for my bath. The sweatpants and shoes were easy, but it hurt like hell when it came to my upper body.

"Can you, uh, help me, please?" I asked, not looking at her to hide my embarrassment at not being able to undress myself. Without a word, she slowly helped me out of my hoody, sling, and t-shirt, and neither of us opened up a wound.

"You got to help me now," she said, breathing heavily. Awkwardly, I stripped her down until she had on nothing except a matching white-lace Victoria's Secret bra and panty set.

"Um. Wow. Perfect. You're absolutely perfect."

"I'm glad you think so, but I'm not," she whispered, blushing.

"No, really, you are. But, um, let's move on. Do you want to turn around while I take off my boxers?"

"I'm a big girl, Dee. I've seen a dick before."

"Okay." Without hesitation, I dropped my boxers and kicked them toward the rest of my clothes. I felt her looking at me from head to toe, and for the first time in a long time I felt self-conscious. Her body was amazing, damn near beyond words. And I was just average. When she finally looked back up into my face, she blushed an even deeper red than before and nibbled slightly on her sexy bottom lip. Then she simply turned around. I didn't know how to take that, and after a few seconds I started to climb into the tub.

"I need you to unhook my bra."

That stopped my leg mid-stride. Luckily I'd honed the skills necessary to unhook a bra with one hand with blinding speed in my youth, and it came back to me now so that before the sentence was out of her mouth, I had the job done. I heard her gasp when I slid the soft fabric down her shoulders and turned her around to face me. Pushing through the pain, I used both hands to ease her panties to the floor, allowing her to step out of them while I took in the intoxicating aroma of her body. She smelled like honey, and I wanted to know if she'd taste the same, but something kept me from exploring this option. Stepping back, I took a thorough look at her stunning body as she stood boldly before me, her eyes smoky with desire and fear of the unknown. Taking her hand, I helped her into the Jacuzzi, and after grabbing one washcloth, I followed her lead.

"Why are you so quiet?"

"I'm nervous, and a little scared, honestly. I mean, I don't even know you, but I'm sitting in your tub completely naked."

"Well, what do you want to know about me?"

"I don't know, Dee. You know what I'm saying, though. I want to be here. I want. I don't know if I should."

"Do you know what I want?"

"What?"

"I want to know what would make you happy."

For the first time, I saw a crack in the wall she'd put up around herself, and just the tiniest bit of vulnerability came out. The conversation flowed easily from that point. We talked about everything from past relationships to politics and sports, then deeper still with questions delving into my world of the past two decades. All the while we bathed each other, the sexual tension so thick it was almost unbearable at times. I wanted her, and I knew it was mutual, but something inside me told me it would mean more to wait.

"Why?" she asked when I was drying her off.

"Why what?"

"Why didn't you make love to me? Being in the water would've made it possible for both of us. I mean, call me old fashioned, but you're the man, so I assumed you'd make the first move. Do you not want me anymore?"

"No, sweetheart, it's nothing like that. It's just right now, trust is a big thing for me. More than your body, I want you: your trust, loyalty, and eventually your love. Those things are all very serious, and they don't come easy, so I wanted to take it slow and resist the anticipation to blow your back out." I told her, smiling and turning her back around so I could look into those captivating eyes.

"Do you really mean that?"

I let my actions speak for themselves and lowered my mouth to hers, kissing her tenderly while pulling her against my naked body so she could feel my skin burn with pure desire for her. I felt her arms snake around my neck and pull me deeper into the mystic and wonder we were creating with only a kiss. There was so much promise in the passion we shared that I knew I'd lose myself totally if I didn't back away now.

"Its okay, baby. I want you, too." She caressed my dick with the softest hands I'd ever felt.

"Mm. Come on, baby, don't make this any more difficult. Patience. I promise it'll be worth it." I kissed her one more time and sat her down on the bed so I could massage lotion into her sensual skin. When I looked up, she had her face set in a sexy pout, making clear her disappointment in me.

"Out of all the niggas in the metropolitan, I gotta get one of the last hopeless romantics."

"Just all the adventures and stories we will tell our kids someday."

At that comment, she pulled the leg back that I'd been working on and took the lotion from my hands.

"I can do it," she said cooley.

"Did I say something wrong, Ramona?"

"No."

"Look, don't bullshit me, keep it real. Communication is the cornerstone of any relationship."

"Relationship? We aren't in a relationship."

"We're trying to build one, I thought. Am I wrong?"

"Dee, just— Just leave it alone, alright?"

There was a silent plea in her eyes — and some pain as well — that made me not force the issue. Rising slowly, I wrapped my towel around my waist and went into my closet to find something to wear.

"Hey, Dee, I got some clothes for—"

I knew it was Candy's voice I'd heard, which meant she was in the room face-to-face with a very naked Ramona.

"What the fuck are you doing, bitch?"

By the time I'd made my way out of the closet, Candy had dropped the shopping bags and was moving toward Ramona with what I recognized as my pistol in her hands.

"Candy, don't."

Hearing my voice, she spun around, but seeing me with only a towel on sent her expression from anger to murderous intent. One clear thought came to my mind with the force of a thunder clap: Kiara had set this in motion.

"You fucked this bitch!" she screamed, training the gun back on the visibly-shaken Ramona.

"No, Candy, I didn't. Calm down and stop waving that pistol before it goes off."

"It's gonna go off, alright. Right in the stinking-ass bitch's brain. I can't believe you fucked her."

It was obvious to me that being calm wasn't gonna defuse the situation.

"Hold up, slim, ain't you fucking my sister? What right do you have to say who I can fuck? And I just told your ignorant ass I ain't had sex with her anyway! Now put that muthafuckin' gun down or be prepared to shoot me, too!"

These words got her attention, but I saw her pain underneath the anger, and it hurt me. I really did care about her, and I had to make her understand that before things got worse.

"Candy, you know how I feel about you. I'm not saying that I'm not developing feelings for Ramona, because I have, but one doesn't take away from the other. Do you love Kiara?"

"Yes."

"Do you love me?"

"You know that I do."

"Okay, but we both know that there's a difference between loving someone and being in love. Are you in love with me?"

"Dee, I'm in love with both of you," she replied, defeat etching the lines in her young face, but the gun never wavered.

"Ramona, take one of the bags of clothes into the bathroom and get dressed."

She looked warily at Candy, but slowly got up and did as I told her, locking the door behind her.

"Come here," I told her, opening my arms and holding her close while she cried.

"Baby girl, I know the feeling to have your heart pulling you in two different directions. I know what it's like to love so much that it seems like a gift and a curse, but you want it anyway. I'm not saying I don't have feelings for you, and I know that whether I want to or not, I'ma end up loving you. What I'm saying is don't let our love destroy you. Think about this. I called Keyz up here right before we got into the Jacuzzi and told her to send someone shopping for Ramona. Why did she send you? Because she knew you'd come up here and see only God knows what, but on my word as a gangsta, we didn't sleep together."

"Why not?"

"It's complicated. All you need to know is that nothing has changed how I feel about you, but you need to learn to control you emotions, because my sister ain't no fool."

"It's just that, with everything going on and Dee, you almost died in my arms. Do you know what that would've done to me? Do you know what seeing you shot did to me? I almost lost you, so how can you expect me not to want to be with you every waking moment?"

Looking into her eyes, I knew she meant every word she said, and that she really did love me. I wiped the tears from her face and kissed her gently.

"I'm here, I'm not going anywhere, okay? I've gotta get ready for this meeting, but I'll make sure that I find a way to see you tonight. That's cool with you?"

"Yes, baby," she replied, kissing me again and tucking the gun into her jeans as she left the room.

"Whew. Alright, Ramona, you can come out."

I turned to my closet, pulling out some black slacks, a black button-up, and some black gators, preparing to get on my Nimo Brown kit, minus the testimony. When I came back out, she was sitting on the bed looking good enough to eat in some tight, stone-washed jeans, a white halter top that obviously didn't require a bra, because she damn sure ain't have one on, and some baby blue and navy blue Air Force Ones. She didn't need makeup, because her natural beauty was enough to stop traffic, and those sexy black eyes set the mood off right. The only problem was the look of death she was giving me. Putting on my Gucci cologne, I turned to see her sitting in the exact same spot with the same exact look on her face. My medication was wearing off, and the pain was back swift and hard, which meant hers should be, too. Oh yeah, this was about to get ugly. Slowly, I made my way to her side of the bed and sat down, taking her hands in mine.

"I'm sorry."

"For?"

"For what happened with Candy, and even before that, for whatever I said that upset you."

"Let's deal with the last issue first: that girl is over the fucking moon for you, and as you can tell, that can be dangerous. So what happens when we — or when you — start seeing someone exclusively?"

"What do you suggest I do?"

"It's not up to me, but either you need to be with her or not. The friends with benefits shit ain't working."

"Do you want to be with me?"

"That brings us back to the first issue. Devaughn, I— I can't have kids. Before you ask, the doctors don't know why, and it wasn't due to some trauma. I mean, I'm only thirty. There's a specialist in Ohio, and I'm saving my money. I just didn't want you to get your hopes up for nothing."

The tears were coming in great waves, her body shaking with the sobs she was still trying to hold in. I pulled her to me and let her get it all out, stroking her back, but not saying a word for the moment. I knew how hollow words could seem without actions, so for now I just wanted to show her I was here. Her revelation was a lot to digest, but it didn't make me want her any less. In fact, it made me want her more. She made me want to be her everything, and I knew I could be if the opportunity presented itself.

"Baby, listen, I'm not searching for a baby mama. I'm searching for a soul mate and companion to complete me in every way. Don't misunderstand, because I understand the burden that you have to carry, but what I'm saying is that I want you for you, and no matter what happens, we'll face it together. Our Happily Ever After can be whatever we make it, as long as we build on the right foundation. So, can we try?"

"Try what?"

"Us. Will you have dinner with me tonight?"

This got a laugh out of her as she pulled back, wiping the tears from her eyes.

"Nigga, we just finished bathing each other, and I've told you more secrets than I have my priest altogether. So yes, I'll have dinner with you."

"Thank you." I gave her a quick kiss and stood to go out the door.

"Where are you going?"

"I've got a meeting, but it shouldn't take more than an hour. Don't worry, I'll be back."

"Dee, you just had major surgery, do you really think you need to be worried about business right now?"

"This ain't business. This is personal, and I've got to handle it, because if I don't, I'm not gonna walk away so lucky next time."

"So what am I supposed to do?"

"We've got a swimming pool, movie theatre, gym, sauna and Jacuzzi, and a big-ass library. I'm sure you can find something to do."

"Can't I just come with you?"

"Sure. Once we're married and you can't testify against me."

"Is that a proposal?"

"If you want it to be."

With that, I walked out of the room and took the elevator to the conference room. When I walked in, I had flashbacks of the incidents that had taken place what seemed like a million years ago. The first was the killing that started the unthinkable, and then there was Candy, right here on this very table I was standing in front of. When I looked to where she was standing by the door, I could tell by the smile on her face that she was thinking the exact same thing I was.

"Stay focused nigga," Keyz said, dropping into the chair next to mine. I didn't like her tone, but decided to let it go. Focusing.

"Report," I said, taking my own seat. My two-star general Blood Money spoke first.

"Everything Shine in D.C., Maryland, and Norfolk has been neutralized and taken over. It's only EMU merchandise moving through these areas. We had a few Shine niggas willing to flip because they didn't like their leadership anyway, but once we got word that you'd been shot, we slaughtered everyone and their families."

"Body count?"

"Somewhere north of eighty."

"Lil' Trey, report."

"We took over the Bronx."

"Body count?"

"170."

"Dirty Red, report."

"It's just us and Valentine in North Carolina. We need more soldiers to help in Texas, though."

"Is Valentine helping?"

"Yes."

"Fine, but tell the men I want them to be wary of anyone who ain't EMU until I determine friend from foe. What's the body count in NC?"

"Fifty."

"Gentlemen, I know you were made aware that I was shot by them Shine niggas. However, what you weren't told is that my big homie orchestrated the hit. I'm sending word to the counsel now about what has happened, but make no mistake, everybody involved is living on borrowed time. This changes nothing for us, but our homies need to know that nigga ain't in our lineup. He's to be watched and not trusted by any means. Ain't a muthafucka alive that can say I ain't Blood, and anybody who tries will be dealt with. Keep in mind that by them coming for me, they're coming for you, too. Be ready for anything."

Chapter 8

Drama

Days turned into weeks, and weeks turned into a bloody month. The body count continued to rise, but now it was a three-way, because I was fighting two very worthy opponents. For the most part Shine was almost eliminated because, as they say, kill the head and the body will fall. Even though I was winning in that area, going against by big homie had turned the whole tidewater into a warzone the likes of which hadn't been seen since the '70s and '80s. My only real advantage had come from the fact he didn't know I had numbers that strong in his territory, and every time he peeked his head out of his hiding place, I had niggas ready to take it off his shoulders. For the most part I'd spent my time healing and getting acquainted with legitimate businesses we owned. I met with business partners and learned the tricks of the trade for washing all my dirty money. It was almost like going back to school.

All the kids had started school with the exception of Deshana, who was my right hand, but nobody went anywhere without plenty of security. Sometimes my kids complained that they were more guarded than the president, but anything less wasn't an option. My ex had transitioned quite well into the lap of luxury, thoughts of Craig escaping her mind. Jordyn was a different story, and every time I came around to visit, she gave me the saddest look before asking me if I had any news about her dad. It broke my heart, not because he was gone, but because he never deserved such a sweet kid anyway. She didn't want for anything, though, because she was treated no different from her sisters and brother.

Despite the promise we'd made Keyz, Candy and I couldn't stay apart from each other. We were discreet though, because Keyz was a suspicious muthafucka and I would've bet money she had the staff watching us. And no matter what happened with me and Candy, my mind was on me and Ramona getting closer still.

I had finally let her go back to work, and her security detail didn't even look out of place in the courthouse. I didn't have a problem with her working, but she more or less lived with me even though we still hadn't taken it to the next level physically. But I had every intention of rectifying that at the next possible opportunity. I hadn't fully committed to her yet, and a lot of it had to do with the fact danger was still very real and we could be over if I blinked.

We discussed at length the complications of a parole officer being involved with a parolee, but in the face of life and death that became insignificant. We both understood that seizing the day was the only way to go. I still hadn't heard from the counsel, which meant I was out here operating completely on my own and without sanction to do what was necessary. I was a man before I was anything, and as a man I had to stand on the decision I made, regardless of who didn't understand or agreed with it.

"Whatcha doing, Big Head?" Keyz asked, interrupting my thoughts and stretching out on the bed next to me.

"Shit, just thinking about everything."

"How's the shoulder?"

"Like new, but I still ain't playing no basketball for a while."

"My nigga, you weren't that good, anyway."

"Fuck you, Light Skin."

"What you doing, anyway? Don't you have a neighborhood or something to buy?"

"Nope, I took the day off so I could be lazy. Besides, what you been doing all day?"

"You really wanna know?"

"I asked didn't I?"

"Well, uh, I was with DC, Angel, and Candy. They got it poppin'! I'm talking about it was ass, pussy, titties, and toys everywhere! I ain't been fucked that good in a long time."

"Alright, damn, I'm sorry I asked."

"So what time does your wife get here?"

"Fuck you, bitch, but I'm about to go get her in a few minutes. Can I ask you something?"

"You know you can ask anything, nigga."

"Do you think I should marry her?"

"Is the pussy any good?"

That was a question I couldn't answer. I ain't never been the type of nigga to lie on my dick, so I guess the truth was all I had.

"I don't know."

"What you mean, you don't know? Either the shit's some good, mediocre, or slum-age, choose one."

"That's not what I'm saying. I don't know because I ain't fucked her yet."

Her laughter was instantaneous and loud, almost making me push her ass out of the bed.

"Why not?" she asked, getting herself under control and wiping the tears from her eyes.

"Because I knew she was special, and I didn't just want it to be about sex. I've moved on and want to do anything other than make love to her."

"Damn. I guess it is serious, my nigga. My advice is wait until this smoke clears. With all this shit we've got going on, marrying her right now makes her a target. Shit, you've seen *The Godfather*."

I knew she was right, but part of me still wanted to make it official in case I didn't make it through this situation. That wouldn't be fair to anyone, though.

"I gotta go." I got up off the bed and brushed the lint from my jeans. I stepped into my Timbs and grabbed my bulletproof vest from the armoire. After I put it on. I threw a plain white t-shirt on over it, grabbed my .45 and my glock, and turned back to face Keyz, who'd been watching my every move.

"No matter what happens, I want you to take care of her, ya got it?"

"I got you, Big Head. You want me to ride with you?"

"Nah, I'ma fly solo in case we wanna get something to eat. Go back to your freedom session with your nasty-ass."

"Nigga, you just mad that you wasn't invited."

"No doubt." I laughed and left her stretched out on my bed.

Taking the stairs, I made my way to the kitchen, where I found Candy stuffing her face with some BBQ ribs.

"Damn, every time I see you you're eating something with your hungry-ass." I opened the refrigerator and grabbed a half carton of orange juice.

"Forget you, negro, this shit is good and a muthafucka. You need to stop faking and get in where you fit in."

"Nah, I'm good. Hold on a second. Intercom on. Page Eternity to the kitchen. Where you get ribs from, anyway?"

"That's my little secret. Um, where you 'bout to go?" she asked, setting the food down and wiped her hands. I wasn't in the mood to have this argument, so I took a long swallow of orange juice, hoping Eternity would hurry up

"I'm going to pick up Ramona."

"Oh. And then what?"

"I don't know, Candy. Why, what's up?"

"I was kinda hoping me and you could talk for a little while, just kick it, you know?"

"You can talk to me now if it's important. If not, I'll probably be tied up until tomorrow." I wasn't trying to sound cold or anything, but she was getting ready to start this jealousy shit like she wasn't just in a four-ring circus earlier.

"It's like that, is it?"

"Like what, Candy? Come on, don't start that bullshit. Like I don't know what you been doing all day."

"This don't have nothing to do with that."

"Oh, so you can get yours, but if I just wanna kick it with a bitch, I'm a bad guy?"

"Dee, you're not listening—"

"Look, I gotta go. I'll holla at you later," I told her, turning around as Eternity walked into the kitchen.

"You're gonna be a father," she blurted out, stopping me dead in my tracks. I could tell by Eternity's facial expression that she'd heard what I did, making a miscommunication damn near impossible. Slowly, I turned back around until I was facing Candy's bright red face, tears swimming in her eyes.

"Huh?"

"I said you're gonna be a daddy. I missed my period."

"How late are you?"

"Three weeks."

"Have you been to the doctor's or peed on a stick? Anything?"

"My doctor's appointment is tomorrow morning, and I took a home pregnancy test a week ago."

"Okay, and?"

"Dee, you're gonna be a father."

"Holy shit."

"You can say that again," Eternity murmured. My mind was spinning. I couldn't believe what I was hearing. Me, a dad again? Part of me wanted to scream it to the world, but the other part stopped me, because this could only mean disaster when Keyz found out.

"Does she know?"

"Hell no, and I'm not telling her until I absolutely have to."

"Okay, okay. I'ma go with you tomorrow to the doctor. What time is the appointment?"

"11:00 a.m., but you're not mad at me?"

"No, sweetheart, I'm not mad. I knew the risks just like you did, and I've never been the type of nigga to duck my responsibilities."

"That's good to know. Where does that put us, though."

"We're not even about to go there right now, Candy, stay focused. Listen, I gotta go, but we'll talk in the morning, right?"

"Yeah, fine, whatever."

"Candy, don't. I got you, so please don't start tripping. Go lay down somewhere and don't do shit that could hurt that baby or I'ma fuck you up."

"Yes, Daddy."

"See, that's how we got into this situation in the first place," I shook my head as me and Eternity left the house.

As soon as I got in the truck, I began twisting up a blunt, hoping the smoke would alleviate the sudden anxiety I felt. This shit wasn't happening. Not now. I couldn't have any more distractions, and I was a guaranteed dead man. I smoked half the blunt in two hits, already reaching for the bottle of cognac from the bar and using it as a chaser.

"Slow down, Dee. It's not that bad."

"Not that bad? Eternity, my sister's girlfriend, her common-law wife, just said that she's pregnant with my baby, and that's not bad to you? Get the fuck out of here!"

"Well, like you said, you both knew what you were getting into. What're you gonna do?"

"That's the million dollar question, and I only have an idea, but nothing solid."

"Whatever you do, don't tell anyone. And you already know I'm not gonna say shit. If…"

"If, what?" I asked, swallowing half the bottle of potent liquor, enjoying the burn on the way down.

"Well, you kinda promised me something, and you haven't delivered on it."

"Now? You pick now of all times to talk about us making love?"

"I've been patient, Dee, and you know it."

"So, are you telling me that you're gonna blackmail me? Are you sure that's the road you wanna go down?" I whispered, feeling the liquor sitting on my empty stomach and the weed starting to kick in already.

"I was only joking, Devaughn. I'll keep the secret, and you know that. It's just that, you know, that you liked me."

"Of course I like you, and yes, I still want to make love to you, but the timing has just been off. My question to you is what are you expecting after that happens?"

"I'm not expecting anything. I'm a grown woman, and I know the score of the game, so don't feel like you have to hold my hand."

This conversation was making my head hurt worse, and I didn't have to worry about fulfilling the sexual desires of an eighteen-year-old girl. Always thinking with my dick had me in a tight spot now! I rolled another blunt and was halfway through it when we pulled up outside the courthouse.

Picking up the phone, I called and told her I was downstairs and waiting. By the time she got in the truck, the blunt and bottle were gone, and I was slumped in the seat, smoking a cigarette.

"Hey, baby." She kissed me and curled up against me. "What's wrong?"

"Why do you think something's wrong?"

"Because I can taste the liquor and smell the weed, and you're obviously fucked up. So what is it?"

How could I tell her? Even our first conversation about kids hadn't gone anywhere near this subject. So how was I supposed to tell her the one thing that was guaranteed to break her heart? At the same time, I'd always been honest with her.

"Do you wanna go somewhere and eat dinner?"

"No, I'd much rather we went home and got something to eat, especially in your condition. Whatever it is, it must be pretty bad."

"Do you love me, Ramona?"

"You know I do."

"Do you trust me?"

"With my life. What's wrong, Devaughn? You're starting to scare me."

"Eternity, put the window up. And why don't you roll one up real quick?"

"Dee."

"Trust me, baby. Twist up, because this shit ain't just bad, it has the potential to be disastrous."

She didn't object, just took over what she needed and shakily rolled a blunt. While she was doing that, I took a bottle of 151, popped the top, and took a healthy swig. I could feel her eyes on me the whole time, finally grasping the severity of whatever I had to tell her, because even though I took the occasional drink, I never got smashed. Everyone knew the end result when mixing white and dark liquor. She lit her blunt while I lit another cigarette and tried to figure out where to begin.

"Earlier today, I asked Keyz's advice about proposing to you. It's not that I doubt us, I'm simply unsure of how this situation is gonna play out and it wouldn't be fair to make you a widow before you had a proper honeymoon. I know we haven't been together long. I hope you know that I love you completely and that'll never change."

"What is it, baby?"

"Candy's pregnant."

It felt like all the air had been sucked out of the truck, and everything stopped moving. I forced myself to look in her eyes, knowing what I would find, but I wouldn't allow myself to get off easy. Her pain crushed me, and her silence was equally torturous as she continued to smoke without taking her eyes off me. I wanted to touch her, to hold her, but I knew somehow I'd lost my right to do that, and the thought of losing her finally broke the dam of my pent-up emotions. My vision blurred, and I felt the hot tears racing down my face, but I refused to wipe them away. All I could do was tip my bottle back to my lips and hope I could maybe drown my pain, if only for a little while.

"It's yours?"

"Yeah."

"Why are you crying?"

At that question, I looked back at her, and even though she wasn't crying, I could see her pain clearly.

"Because I know I've lost you. I can see your pain as if it were my own, and in a lot of ways it is. The last thing I ever wanted was to hurt you. I'm sorry."

"Does Kiara know?"

"No, I can't tell her. I made her a promise that we wouldn't sleep together anymore."

"Well, she's gonna find out, so then what?"

"I don't know. I don't know anything right now. I didn't even know if I was gonna tell you, but I've never lied to you, and I couldn't start now."

We rode on is a strained silence, her still smoking and I finishing another bottle. Common sense told me that I was completely fucked up, but that didn't stop me from reaching for another bottle of cognac.

"Dee, enough." She gently pushed me back onto the seat and closed the bar.

Too far gone to argue, I settled for trying to roll another blunt.

"Dee, come on, we're home, and Deshana is standing out front, so no more for now."

I didn't want to stop, I just wanted to stop feeling. I stuffed the weed in my pocket and made a clumsy exit when Eternity opened my door.

"S'appenin', Lil' M?"

"Dad, what's wrong?"

"Ain't shit I can't handle. What's good with you?"

"Dad, you're high as a muthafucka and you smell like pure liquor. What the fuck is going on?"

"Leave it alone, Deshana," I said, nodding. "Damn, can't I party with my woman?"

Deshana looked at Ramona, and Ramona shook her head while leading me to the house. I felt like I was on a big-ass rollercoaster, and I just wished the room would stop spinning so I could get off.

"What up, bruh? Dee, are you drunk?"

"A little."

"Fuck no, you're absolutely smashed. Ramona, what happened?"

"Don't ask me, he was more than halfway there by the time he picked me up. Don't worry, I'm taking him up to bed now."

"Dee, when you sober up, I'ma whoop your ass, you stupid muthafucka."

"Bring it, bitch," I slurred, smiling and staggering toward the elevator. When we got on, I thought I might hurl. When we got off, I almost did. Slowly I was half-carried, half-dragged into my room, where they dropped me in a heap on my bed. I felt someone take my shoes off, and then Ramona climbed in bed beside me.

"I'm so sorry, baby," I slurred, taking her in my arms and sighing when she didn't refuse.

"I know."

"I never meant— I love you so much, Ramona. You know that, don't you?"

"Yes, Dee, I know."

I felt the bottom getting ready to give out on this rollercoaster, but I had one more question.

"Baby, can you forgive me?" I waited for her response, but all I heard was her breathing. And then I heard nothing as the floor moved and I dropped into another world.

The nightmare that came this time was different. Somebody I'd never seen or met before was holding a shotgun to my head and accusing me of playing God. I woke up just as he pulled the trigger. Even before I opened my eyes, I could smell the smoke wafting through the air, but instead of the normal, calm affect I was expecting, my stomach lurched in violent protest. Jumping from the bed, I raced into the bathroom and heaved pure alcohol into the toilet until I thought my intestines would come out my mouth. Stumbling to the sink, I brushed my teeth and then stripped, hoping that an ice-cold shower would somehow help at least my physical situation. I stayed under the pumping water until I thought I would be hypothermic, wondering even if that would be better than facing the woman who I knew awaited me on the other side of the door. When I came back into the room, she was sitting on the bed, smoking a blunt and staring off into space.

"Did you sleep?"

"A little."

"What time is it?"

"3:00 a.m."

My heart hurt for what I'd done to her. Just in the way she talked, I could tell if our relationship did survive this, it would take a while before it was ever the same. Still dripping wet, I sat next to her on the bed and took her hand in mine, thankful she didn't push me away, but closed her fingers around mine. I wasn't sure what to say. What would fix this? Fix us? I could tell her I loved her, but she knew that. I could tell her there was no other, but that would be a lie. What did she want to hear from me to make this right? I only hoped she loved me enough.

"I love you."

"I had no reason to doubt that."

"But?"

"Do you want to be with her, Dee?" she asked, facing me and looking me in the eye for the first time.

"I want to be with you."

"For how long, Dee?"

"For however long you'll have me."

She released my hand then, put the blunt in the ashtray, and walked to my armoire. I didn't need to see what she picked up to know what she had in her hand. I hadn't exactly hidden it.

"Whose is this?"

"Yours."

"So why didn't you give it to me? Did you change your mind?"

"No, but what if I die before I can give you everything you deserve?"

"Baby, I worry about you every second we're not together, and God forbid something happens to you, but don't you know that our love wouldn't die with you? I know what you think I want, but what I really want is you."

"For how long?"

"Forever, Dee," she replied, wiping the tears from her face and kissing me.

"Are you sure?"

"This is how sure I am: Devaughn Andre Mitchell, will you be my husband?" she asked, finally opening her hand to reveal the flawless, seven-carat diamond engagement ring that seemed to glow in the dark. Taking it, I slipped it onto her left ring finger, the tears in my eyes making it sparkle even more.

"Yes, love, I will marry you."

Taking her into my arms, I kissed her hard, tasting the salt from our combined tears, but knowing soon they'd be tears of joy. I undressed her in a daze, needing to feel her naked flesh against my own in a way that I'd never needed any woman before. Our breathing came in short gasps as we both fought for a control that was rapidly vanishing, wanting to make love, but deep down needing to become one more than anything else. I felt her intense heat as I rose overtop of her and positioned myself at the threshold of her sacred sweetness, crying out in surprised pleasure at the new sensations I felt when pushing into the tight folds of her juicy wetness. From the first stroke, I heard warning bells of my climax, but I continued to ram into her with enough force to shake the house. Her pleas went from moans to screams until I felt her sink her teeth into my shoulder, sending a primal surge through me that only intensified the spell. She had me falling harder, and still I drove into her gushing pussy, locking my fingers with hers and my teeth to her neck as we savagely ravished each other with passion born of suspense.

"Oh, fuck me, Dee. Take it, it's all yours. Mm, mi amore, give it to me, Papi."

My feelings indescribable, I was in a sexual rage unlike anything I'd experienced. Her moans propelled me on faster and faster, the sound of our skin slapping like gunshots in the night. I could feel her cum, feel her body convulse beneath my steady strokes, but I wanted more. Not missing a beat, I threw both of her legs onto my shoulders and put my hands behind her shoulders, looking at her face and delivering pounding blows that sent her eyes rolling backward.

"Dee! Oh God. Don't — don't stop. You're hitting my G — G spot!"

I could see the shock on her face and felt her cum again almost immediately, sending me spiraling out of control as I released the beast and came so hard my vision blurred.

"Oh, shit," she whispered, both of us gasping for what little air was left in the room. With effort, I was able to climb out of her pussy and collapse next to her, my mind still trying to catch up with the greatest climax I'd ever had in my life. Part of me wanted to drift off into a peaceful slumber, but I was still craving her, and I knew I couldn't rest until my appetite was sated,

"Come here, baby."

"I would, but I don't think I can move."

Sliding my arm under her, I pulled her on top of me.

"Baby, you didn't—?"

"Of course I did."

"So then, why is—"

"Shh," I told her, kissing her gently and moving until I had my dick tucked snugly inside her waiting, hot pussy. Slowly she took over and took our loving to heights unimaginable, both of us letting go completely until we were clinging to each other, making promises of forever. Time moved on, positions switched, but the message remained the same as we made love until the sun came up and we fell asleep holding each other in unconditional love and happiness.

"Mm, baby, you up?"

"I guess if I wasn't, I am now. Why, what's wrong?"

"Nothing."

"What time is it?"

"A little after 10:00 a.m."

"Sweetheart, we just went to sleep. What are you doing up? I know I put this dope dick in you."

"You're so stupid. Last night — this morning — was beautiful. I've never experienced anything like it before. I've just been laying here looking at my ring."

"What's wrong? You don't like it?"

"No, I love it! I just can't believe it's really happening, this moment is surreal."

"It's real, sweetheart, and whenever you set a date, we'll make you officially Mrs. Mitchell."

"What about today?"

"You wanna get married today?"

"Yeah."

This got my attention to where I actually had to open my eyes and look at her. What I saw surprised me.

"Ramona, what's wrong? I see sadness in you that shouldn't be there, if you're really happy and sure, that is."

"I'm happy and I'm sure. But I'm scared."

"Of?"

"Losing you. I mean, there's a lot going on, and I don't know the half of it, plus I can't give you a baby."

"Stop, Ramona. Sweetheart, my love for you isn't based on us making a baby together. You're what I want, and nothing and no one else. Okay?"

"Well, what if— What if I want a baby by you?"

I wasn't sure why, but that thought hadn't occurred to me, knowing it was only natural for a woman to want kids by their husbands.

"Alright, first of all, I don't want you to feel like you have to compete with Candy, because you don't. If it's something you really want, then I can have us in the air and on our way to Ohio within the hour."

"Ya'd really go through that with me?"

"Next question. I'd do anything for you, sweetheart, and you know that."

Her response was to snuggle up against me with her hand on my chest and go back to studying her ring. I knew we had a long road ahead of us, but I'd meant what I said, and I was firmly dedicated to making her happy.

"Hey, Dee?"

"Yeah, baby?"

"I still want to get married today."

"Justice of the Peace?"

"Uh-huh."

"Intercom on. Page Kiara to north wing master suite. Are you sure you don't want a big wedding?"

"You know I don't really have any family in the states, but I would like to have a catholic service in Italy whenever we can get away."

"Whatever you want, babe. Where should we go on our honeymoon?"

"Um, surprise me."

"I think I can do that. When so you wanna leave?"

"As soon as possible."

"What up, Dee? I was wondering if you were awake," Keyz said, she and Candy coming into the room.

"Why, what happened?"

"Uh, we need to talk."

"Just say it. I'm not hiding shit else from Ramona."

The silence was loud and thick, with Keyz and Candy throwing ugly looks at Ramona, who was sitting up, holding the sheet to her chest.

"Well?"

"The counsel contacted us, and you've got a holographic meeting with them at 1:00 p.m."

"Okay, that's what's up?"

"That's not all."

"Spit it out, Kiara."

"Look, are you sure we can trust her?"

"Yeah."

"I mean damn, Dee, you just met the bitch," Candy spat nastily.

Before I could respond, Ramona was up out of bed butt-naked, hands on her hips and her lips yelling.

"Who you calling bitch? I let your little young-ass slide one time when you pulled a gun on me, but don't take that for weakness, because I'll fuck you up, bitch!"

"Come get some!"

"Whoa, hold the fuck up!" I yelled, pulling my boxers on as fast as I could.

"Y'all muthafuckas need to cool out with all that dumb-ass shit, because I ain't got the time for it."

"You ain't nothing but a piece of pussy, Ramona, and as soon as he gets bored with you, your ass is gone." Candy rubbed her stomach slowly with a smug and satisfied smile.

Keyz didn't notice. She was too busy looking as what Candy hadn't seen. Both women stared at each other, knowing the secret the three of us shared. At first it was evident that Candy had gotten to Ramona in a major way, but when I saw Ramona's smile, I knew what was coming next. Casually, she coughed into her hand. The rock I'd given her was big enough to stop traffic, and that's exactly what it did.

Keyz's look wasn't one of surprise, but I couldn't put my finger on what it was. She was almost smiling, like she had a secret. Candy's mouth was open in shock as she looked back and forth between the ring and me, not believing what was going on. There was no room for doubt, because Ramona's radiant smile said it all

"Dee, what's that on her finger?"

"What does it look like? It's an engagement ring. We're getting married,"

"How? How? When?"

"Ramona," I said before she could respond, "go get in the shower so we can get ready."

"Nope, I'm gonna walk around smelling like the love we made until sunrise," she replied, smiling on her way to the closet to pick out her outfit.

"Dee, how could you?" Candy screamed, spinning around and running from the room.

"Shit."

"She'll get over it. Congratulations, Big Head. I hope you both are very happy."

"Do you mean that, Kiara? Because see, I'm starting to get the feeling that you're enjoying other people's misery. You knew Candy's history with men, but you still let me sleep with her. Why?"

"Look, my nigga, I was just trying to do you a favor. It ain't my fault she caught feelings for you."

"You're a woman, right?"

"And?"

"So, any woman knows that if you have sex with someone more than once, feelings become involved. You can't think like a fucking dude all the time."

"Well, if you know so much, then why did you fuck her?"

"Because I liked her, dummy! Man, fuck all that, what else is going on?"

By now, Ramona had on an all-white, strapless Dolce and Gabana dress that flowed gracefully to her feet and some matching high-healed sandals. She was sitting on the bed listening intently.

"Our people ran into somebody who believes he can help with our problem. He says he did time with you about eleven years ago."

"Who?"

"He said to tell you Four Tray Amn."

A slow smile spread across my face as the face of who she was talking about came clearly into view.

"How do I get in touch with him?"

"Here's the number." She handed me a slip of paper that I passed to Ramona, who stuck it in her ample cleavage.

"Alright, I'll call him. Now I gotta get dressed so we can go."

"There's more, Dee."

"Okay, what else?"

"Dee, I love you, and I trust your judgment, but are you absolutely sure that you wanna keep talking in front of her?"

I turned to gaze on my lovely fiancé, seeing the feelings I had for her mirrored in her eyes, but I knew they'd be there. In all the time we'd been together, I'd never hidden who I was or what I was capable of, and I wouldn't start now.

"Before she goes on, I want you to know something, Ramona."

"Okay."

"I won't ever lie to you, but don't ever ask me a question you don't want the answer to."

"I understand, Dee."

"Go ahead, Keyz." I never took my eyes off of the woman sitting in front of me.

"The cops searched the funeral home, and they're asking questions. Apparently the Taylor family has been missing for a while now."

I didn't say anything, just watched her look transition from shock to suspicion and waited on her to speak.

"The Taylor family. Dee, what's the names of the girls that sent you to prison?"

"Taylor."

And there it was. Suspicion vanished and was quickly replaced by realization, but under that was something she had to question, because it didn't seem possible.

"Ramona."

"You— You went to prison for twenty years for a crime that you didn't commit, and I'm not gonna ask because I don't want to know, but I remember when we first started getting to know each other and I really thought you were holding back, a statement that you made."

"What?"

"You've never killed anyone who didn't deserve to die. I believe you, which allows me to understand you better."

"So, do you still want to, you know?"

"Next question."

Smiling, I pulled her to her feet and kissed her thoroughly, only stopping when Keyz cleared her throat loud enough to remind us we had an audience.

"Mm. Anything else?"

"Nope. What do you want with me?"

"Oh, um, we're getting married."

"No shit. I'm still stuck on that big-ass rock."

"No, I mean we're going to get married right now."

"Stop playing."

"I'm dead-ass serious. Do you want to come?"

"Um, actually, I heard Candy talking about a doctor's appointment in, like, half an hour to Eternity, so—"

"Candy's a big girl, she can go to the doctor by herself. So come on, K. I need you."

"Who else is coming?"

"I don't know. I was thinking about the diva squad, but I don't think that's gonna go over very well."

"Fuck nah, nigga, Deshana might shoot Ramona. You know she wants you to get back with Mikko."

"Not in my lifetime. Will you be my best man?"

"Fuck you, nigga. Yeah, I'll go. Ramona, you're not bisexual, are you?"

"Sorry, just dick," she replied, blushing and smiling.

"That's a damn shame, because you're a sexy-ass woman."

"Alright, enough with that shit! Tell Eternity to bring the truck around in fifteen minutes."

"Alright, I'll be downstairs." She looked Ramona up and down one more time and left the room.

"Your sister is weird."

"I know. Come here, Mrs. Mitchell."

"Yes, Mr. Mitchell."

"Seriously, baby, are you sure you're okay with the life I lead?"

"Only if you make me a promise?"

"And what's that?"

"That you'll retire before I have to bury you," she whispered, laying her head against my chest. Could I really see leaving the game, even for her? I never envisioned me retiring from my way of life. I'd always thought that in the end I'd die like I'd lived. Yet now I had so much more to live for. Only time would tell.

"As long as you promise to keep loving me."

"I think I can manage that."

"Promise?"

"I promise, Devaughn."

"Alright, come on so I can get dressed."

I let her pick out my clothes, and she chose a double-breasted, charcoal grey, pinstriped suit with a white shirt, burgundy tie, and matching burgundy gators. She even dressed me, which was more fun for me than she could even imagine, but I knew I'd return the favor later when I undressed her. Going to the safe, I took out $100,000 and put it in one of the empty bags that her new clothes had come in.

"What's that for?"

"Gotta make a quick stop on the way back."

"Ooh, so mysterious."

Laughing, we walked out the door arm in arm and took the stairs down to the foyer where Keyz and Eternity waited.

"Well, let's do this."

"We got a problem, Dee."

"Now what?"

"You've been summoned by your children, and if I had to guess, I'd say that Candy told Deshana what's going on, although she doesn't know it's going down now."

"I'll deal with that when we get back. Let's go." opened the door and ushered everyone out into the bright mid-morning sunlight. As soon as we stepped out and closed the door, we were ambushed by the entire diva squad, including Jordyn.

"Where you going, Dad?" Latavia asked first, making it known that she was the leader in the inquisition.

"La-La, don't start."

"What do you mean, don't start, Dad? Don't we have a right to know what you're doing?" Day-Day asked, hands on her hips and looking so much like her mother my heart hurt.

"That's not what I'm saying, and you know it."

"So what are you saying, then?" Jordyn asked, never taking her eyes off Ramona.

"I'm saying I love you all, and that's not gonna change, no matter who I marry."

"But Dad, you barely even know her." Latavia threw dirty looks at a smiling Ramona.

"Baby, I do know her, but more than that, I know love — real love — and this is it."

"What about Mom?" This question came from the only person I knew it would. All her life, Deshana had been told of the epic love me and her mother shared, even going so far as to tell her she was the only planned pregnancy. I guess it was only natural that she wanted to see that firsthand.

"Sweethearts, I will always love your mother. She gave me all of you, and a long time ago she helped me learn how to become a man, and I thank her for that, too. But no matter how much I love her, I know that we can't be together anymore because we will only destroy one another. I don't want that, and I don't want any of you to see that. Deshana, do you remember what you asked me after what you saw that first day?"

"Yeah."

"Then please understand why I can't go back to her."

The look in her eyes told me she understood, but she wished things could be different.

"Come on, Ramona."

"Wait, Dee. Listen, I know you ladies don't like me, but in all fairness, you don't know me. I won't dwell on that, though. What I will do is tell you why I'm gonna marry this man today. He is by far the sweetest and most genuine man I've ever met, but he doesn't use material things to show these qualities. He's considerate, thoughtful, and loving, but you already know this. Do you know what I love most? I love that he's not perfect, and he's real about that shit. I love that he treats me like a queen, not because of who I am, but because I'm a woman, period. I love that he's willing to sacrifice everything for those he loves. I love that he loves me for me. Despite everything, he still loves me for me. He's everything I've ever wanted in a man, and I can't see myself living without him. That's why I asked him to marry me."

There wasn't a dry eye in the circle as she professed her love for me, making my heart swell even more with my love for her. Regardless of what happened, I knew that for today I was making the best decision of my life.

"Can I see your ring?" Jordyn asked, stepping up to Ramona and taking the hand she offered.

"Damn," the little girl said, causing everyone to laugh.

"J-Baby, how old are you?" I asked.

"I'm thirteen. How do you know my nickname?"

"I gave it to you." I cast a knowing glare at Keyz, because that was the same age she was when I gave her the name.

"Are we invited?" Latavia asked.

"Do you wanna come?"

A quick glance at her sisters and the vote was unanimous. "Yes."

"Everybody in the truck, then."

An hour later, I was basking in the glow of my new bride and listening to my kids argue about where we should honeymoon. Like they were going. I couldn't help but to keep looking at Ramona and smiling to myself. I had a sure winner on my hands who I knew I didn't deserve her, but I'd spend forever trying to make her happy. There was only one thing missing.

"Keyz, what time is it?"

"It's 12:00 p.m. We got an hour."

Leaning forward, I rattled off an address to Eternity, who'd been quiet like she was stuck in a world all her own. I knew I was gonna have to talk to her sooner than later. I couldn't wait to see the look on Ramona's face when we pulled up at the house, but since we had fifteen more minutes, I decided I'd get some business done.

"Give me that number I gave you."

"Get it yourself," she purred seductively. Without hesitation, I dove in between her gorgeous breasts, kissing her firmly in the process.

"Damn, nigga, you can at least wait until we get home."

"Fuck you." I pulled out the number, grabbed the phone, and dialed.

"Who dis?"

"Let me speak to Tonio."

"Who dis?"

"Dis Big."

"Oh shit, what's good, bro?"

"Ain't shit, my nigga. What's real good with you?"

"Shit, you already know, getting that money by any means necessary."

"You know I'm with that. I been hearing your name ring bells, my nigga, on some real big boy shit."

"Come on, bro, you knew I don't bullshit 'bout getting this paper. If you was smart, you would've got down. Shit, you knew me when we were just an idea."

"I doubt, but you know I had things going on at the time."

"I can respect that. Matter fact, I heard what happened to you when you was down here. I tried to slide through and see you at the hospital, but you had some mean security, not to mention the police."

"Yeah, shit was wild, but I'm still breathing."

"Yeah, I hear that. I also heard that you trying to stop that other nigga from the same?"

"More or less. Why, what's good?"

"Here lately with everything that's going on, he ain't really been able to get out and about, so I'd start to supply his whole team with work."

"So, what's it gonna take for me to holla at this nigga?"

"Since I fuck with you, I'm just asking if you pick up the tab."

"And how much is that?"

"300."

"When?"

"Wherever's good for you."

"We'll play it by ear, but I'll be in touch with you tomorrow sometime."

"Alright nigga, keep ya head down."

"You do the same, my nigga." I hung up, already contemplating my next move. I wanted to leave and go on my honeymoon tonight, but if I could handle this situation, then I needed to do that first. Slowly, the truck eased to a stop on a quiet suburban street in front of an all-white, three-story townhouse.

"Dad, are you sure about this?" Latavia asked, immediately recognizing the house and knowing who was inside.

"This is the last piece of the puzzle, La La, and I've never been surer about anything. Y'all just post up out here, because we won't be long. Come on, babe." I grabbed the bag and Ramona's hand as we hopped out.

"Who lives here, Dee?"

"Be patient. sweetheart." I rang the bell and braced myself when I heard footsteps. I needed something for me to hold onto, taking my wife's hand in mine and gathering the strength I needed. On the other side of that door was the only woman in the free world who could bring me to my knees with a simple look.

"Well, well, look who finally decided to pay me a visit. I ought to whoop your ass, boy, and you know that, don't you?"

"Yes, ma'am."

"Uh-huh. Well, don't just stand there, get in here and give me a hug, fool."

Passing the bag to a confused Ramona, I swept the little woman off her feet and hugged her tightly until she made me put her down.

"Bring yourself in here and close the door. Letting out all the air conditioning."

We did as we were told and followed her into the den, where we sat on the couch facing her.

"Ain't this here the woman they tried to say you killed in broad daylight last month? Your probation officer?"

"Yes, ma'am. But as you can see, that was some complete bullshit. She's alive and well."

"Hmm. Who's trying to kill you this time?"

"It doesn't matter, you're not in any danger."

"Oh, I know. I'm not worth it. I wish a muthafucka would try me!"

"God rest his soul," I laughed. At seventy-seven years old, she still had spunk and a fire what let everyone know that on a good day, she wasn't to be fucked with.

"Okay, well, I can see that the pretty little thing ain't dead, which means you won't be going back to prison right now, but why did you bring her here?"

"Because, Momma, she needed to meet you."

Ramona's gasp was loud when it was finally revealed who this firecracker of a lady was sitting in front of her.

"I can't believe you brought me here without telling me who I was meeting." She hit me on the arm and cursed at me so fast in fluent Italian that I couldn't catch a word. My mother and I exchanged knowing looks, and both of us laughed.

"Well, Devaughn, you've only brought one other female to meet me, and you married that dummy, so what are you here to tell me?"

"Well Momma, Ramona is nothing like Mikko, and I do love her very much. And, well, show her, baby."

Looking positively petrified, she held out her ring finger for my mother to see.

"Damn. That's a hell ova rock. Is it real?"

"Come on, Ma. Stop joking, you know I ain't doing shit halfway."

"So, is this your engagement, or are you already married. Ah. That blush means you're married. Alright, boy, go on upstairs and find something to so while us womenfolk talk."

"Yes, ma'am. Don't be scared, sweetheart," I whispered to her before I left her in the clutches of my loving, yet unforgiving mother. I was her favorite, and she knew about my heartbreaks, so she'd do everything she could to prevent another one. I had time to explore the home that had become but a distant memory to me. I could still remember when she first bought it. Me and my girlfriend at the time had christened it with screams of passion echoing from bare walls. Now the walls held pictures of faraway places, and even some of me a lifetime ago. A lot of things were just like I remembered, but I'd expected that since she barely changed anything that worked for her. Stopping in the kitchen, I made a quick peanut butter and jelly sandwich, grabbed a diet coke, and made my way back downstairs. I walked into the den, where I found them laughing over some old photographs.

"Come on, Ma, not the baby pictures. I'm almost forty."

"So? And who told you to drink on of my sodas?"

"Relax, Mom, this and the sandwich are for you."

"Oh, thank you, baby."

"Listen, Ma, we gotta run. I got some business to handle before we get this honeymoon underway."

"Business, huh? Ramona, I'ma tell you a secret: all you gotta do is give him a swift kick in the ass to keep him in line."

My wife laughed at that. I gave my mom a hug and a kiss, promising to come back soon. Ramona stood and did the same, and we headed for the door.

"You forgot you bag, Devaughn."

"That's for you, Momma. If you need anything, just let me know."

"Goddamn!" I heard her say when she opened the door and stepped back outside. We'd almost made it to the truck when she called me back to her.

"Yes, ma'am?"

"How much?"

"$100,000."

"That's too much, Devaughn."

"Nothing is too much for you, Ma. Enjoy yourself, okay?"

"Baby."

"Yes, ma'am?"

"I like her. She's a keeper, and she's tough. Make sure you treat her right and keep her safe."

"Yes, ma'am. I love you, Momma."

"You too, baby."

Getting back in the truck, I heard my daughters arguing about where me and Ramona should live once we moved out of Keyz's house, but it seemed far away because my mind was thinking about the smiling woman in my arms.

"What did she say, Big Head?"

"She told me to keep her and treat her right."

"Really?"

"Yeah."

"Damn, Ramona, what did you say to her? His mom don't like nobody."

"Keyz, that's a secret. I can't even tell my husband."

"Oh, I have ways of making you talk."

The rest of the ride home we all laughter and jokes, making plans for family vacations, and forgetting about all the negative shit for as long as possible. When we got home, I carried my bride over the threshold, but I damn near dropped her at the stairs at the sight of Candy standing in the foyer with her arms across her chest and her foot tapping.

"Dee, I need to talk to you. Now."

Everyone was silent, just staring at the obviously heartbroken woman and not knowing what to expect. I slowly sat Ramona down and placed her behind me, not knowing if gunplay was on the menu for today.

"Alright, come on."

"Dee, you've got a meeting in ten minutes. You know that you can't miss that. She can wait."

"I got this, Keyz." I took Candy's hand and led her to the elevator. Neither of us spoke until we were in the conference room, sitting down.

"What's up, Red?"

"How could you, Dee? How could you ask her to marry you?"

"Because I'm in love with her, Candy."

"So you don't love me?"

"You know I love you, and I love the baby inside you, too."

"Then why choose her over me?"

"You chose Keyz, that's your partner, so how is it my fault that I felt entitled to happiness?"

"Because you should've known that I would have chosen you. I'm carrying your fucking child, Dee!"

"Candy, listen to me, my love for you is still there, and it won't change, but I made a decision to be with Ramona, and if you really love me, you'll respect that."

"Respect that? Respect that? I don't know how, Dee, when everything inside me is screaming for you."

I didn't know what else to say. *I'm sorry* was such a hollow platitude that I wouldn't really attempt it right then. I didn't have anything else to offer in the way of comforting words.

"What did the doctor say?"

"I'm six weeks pregnant, and the baby is healthy."

"Are you gonna have it?"

"Do you want me to?"

"Yes."

"Why?"

"Because I love you, and our child was created in love."

"I'm gonna have the baby, Dee, but do me a favor."

"Anything."

"Stop saying you love me. It hurts too much," she replied, dejectedly rising and leaving the room. I was stuck. Today was one of the best and worst days in my life, but the scary part was that it wasn't over.

I was jolted from my thoughts by the announcement of an incoming holographic projection seconds before I came face-to-face with a legend.

"Peace, Almighty," I said humbly and respectfully.

"Peace, young blood. You know who I am?"

"Mr. Inferno."

"More or less. And since you know that I know you, understand the great honor you're receiving by talking to me."

"I do, big homie."

"Alright, then let's get to the point. The shit that you did was reckless, and you did it without permission, which is a direct violation. However, you were operating within the rules and regulations when you reacted on blatant disrespect. In light of that circumstance, it has been decided that the punishment Skino handed down was unjust, meaning you've been taken off of the wall of shame. The only problem with that is that Skino doesn't agree. Rather than get involved, we've decided to let you two handle it. Dee, in the ring, dog gonna fight, dog off the leash, dog gonna bite. Whatever the outcome, you both have to live with those consequences. Now, as far as the Shine situation, that's over. Understand that there will not be another bullet exchanged between you and any Shine homie, or the whole nation will devour you. Is that understood?"

"More or less, the territory you took will remain yours, but you will make contributions to the nation accordingly. You will also relinquish your control over the Bronx, effective immediately. Your violation has cost you $5,000,000, to be transferred by 5:05 p.m. today. Any questions?"

"No."

"Oh, by the way, depending on how the situation with you and Skino plays out, there's a meeting next month up here, and one of you will be required to attend."

"Understood."

"Peace, Blood."

"Peace, Almighty."

And with that, the image was gone, leaving just me and my thoughts to contemplate the future for me and mine.

"Intercom on. Page Kiara to the conference room." I actually came off better than I could've hoped. It could've easily gone the other way, because no one man was bigger than the organization, and even though I would've and had gone to war, I held no illusions about the outcome if the counsel didn't agree with my actions.

"What happened?" she asked, rushing into the room. I explained the whole conversation and the counsel's decisions, making sure she understood the orders that had to be issued and followed. One war was over, But the other...

"So, what are you gonna do?"

The smile I gave her caused her to shudder and take a step back from me.

"Do? I'm gonna kill him."

Chapter 9

Payback

"Stop. Stop. Mm, shit. You're killing me, baby. Wait, wait. I'm—Oh shit!"

"You're welcome."

"Thank you," I panted, trying to catch my breath and slow down my heart, because it felt like it was gonna burst.

"That wasn't fair, Ramona. You tortured me on purpose."

"Oh, nigga, you did the same shit to me last night. You had me climbing the walls and screaming and shit. I bet your sister heard us way on the other side of the house. Now, you know I gotta brush my teeth."

"Why?"

Her smile was dazzling. "You didn't think I'd waste all that good protein, did you?"

"You mean?"

"Of course I swallowed it. You're my husband!" I pulled her to me and kissed her, the heat of her mouth turning me on, making me want to forget all else and make love to her until she couldn't walk.

"And you're my wife, and you never see me brush my teeth after I'm finished snacking on those tasty goodies you got. I love all the flavors of you, especially when you cum."

"Oh, you do?"

"Let me show you."

In a matter of minutes, I made her pay for the pleasurable pain she'd just given me, nibbling and sucking on her pussy until all she could do was hold onto me and beg.

Once my mission was complete, I left her lying in the bed, smoking a blunt. Satisfaction etched in the lines of her face and the glow of her sweat-covered body. I couldn't erase the smile off my face while I took a quick shower and tried to focus on when I would have the traitorous muthafucka Skino hanging from his balls. I could've easily sent some niggas to do the job for me, but it went beyond personal. I had to have him. I'd let my glocks tie up the loose ends of those in his circle.

Finishing my shower, I came out of the bathroom to find her holding a towel in one hand and a fresh blunt for me in the other. I took the blunt, but she pulled the towel back from me. I relaxed while she dried me off from head to toe. At the rate we were going, I might have never left the bedroom, let alone the house.

"Baby, don't start. You know I gotta get ready to leave."

"I know, I know. I'm just trying to save time. Enjoy your smoke and I like to do this, okay?"

"Whatever you say sweet. See, you not — not playing fair," I mumbled, my hand inadvertently going to her curls as she took my dick into her mouth until it disappeared. I held on for dear life, biting my lip until I tasted my own blood while she devoured me. She showed me no mercy, and when I tried to back up, she grabbed onto my ass cheeks, making me fuck her face. With the technique of a porn star combined with no gag reflex, she made quick work of me, and before I knew it I had dropped the blunt I was holding and gripped her head tightly as my knees buckled.

"You're so — so damn nasty. Why you do me like that?"

"You ain't always going to have the last word, sweetheart. Now get dressed," she ordered, smacking me on the ass and prancing into the bathroom.

I didn't move until I heard the shower come on. Picking my blunt back up, I relit it and strolled to my closet feeling like a natural-born king. I'd not known a woman before that I craved physically every time I saw her. And honestly, at my age I was surprised to be getting it back as fast as I was. It was her. There was no other explanation needed, because the reality was that my wife made me feel like I was young again. Still smiling, I pulled out some light blue polo jeans, a plain black t-shirt, and my black air force ones, and brought everything to the bed. Grabbing another empty shopping bag, I went to the safe and took out $300,000, my .45, the Taurus 9mm, and a stack of ammo. With the money in the bag, I sat it by the door and proceeded to get dressed. I'd just finished tying my shoes when the shower turned off. Knowing Ramona would be out here naked and wet in moments was making it difficult to focus. I looked up and there she stood, only wrapped in a towel, all wet and naked.

"You're not going to let me leave then, are you?"

"You can do whatever you want, baby. And I do mean *whatever* you want."

"See that's — that's bullshit." I tugged and grabbed the towel while taking her in my arms to dry her off. "Seriously, I've gotta get on the road."

"I know," she whispered, turning her head half away from mine and staring out the window.

"Hey. What's wrong?"

"Nothing, I'm okay."

"Don't lie to me, Mona."

"Mona?"

"Yeah, you're my Mona Lisa, priceless and one-of-a-kind."

"I like that, but you a slick muthafucka, and you probably trying to take advantage of me."

"Of course. But why are you trying to change the subject? What's wrong, sweetheart?"

"Do you want to go back to Norfolk? I mean, the police made it clear that they didn't want you back down there, and look what happened last time." She looked at me with tears in her eyes. I had a feeling this was the heart of the problem. Being that we'd promised each other forever, I didn't feel the need to keep secrets, so I'd told her about my trip. I just hadn't told her why I was going.

"Baby, listen to me, everything will be fine, okay? My team knows I'm coming, and they'll be there to meet me as soon as I enter the city. I probably won't even get out of the truck this time, and even though I do trust my niggas, I'm still not willing to put all my business in just anyone's hands."

"Why can't Keyz go? She was handling all the business before you came home, so why can't she step back in and take care of this last loose end?"

"She has a doctor's appointment or something."

"Well, then send someone else!" she shouted as my arms were pulling her over and taking on a life of their own. I hugged her tightly and tried to calm her down while she sobbed, every wail from her mouth pushing me closer to death's door. I didn't want to hurt her, didn't want to do anything that would make her sad, but I didn't know how to explain how important it was to get this over with. I clung to her as she to me, feeling the beating of her heart readily in sync with mine, and let her cry until her sobs turned into whimpers.

"Baby, I promise you that everything will be fine. This trip eliminates the immediate threats to us, and as soon as I'm done, we're gone on our honeymoon for at least a month. I just need you to trust me, sweetheart, and know that your love is what will bring me back. Can you do that?"

"Dee, I'm just so scared. I couldn't take losing you. Look how long it took to find you."

"I know, and I love you with everything that I am or ever hope to be. I'm never going anywhere." I could feel that the quivering in her body had stopped, but she still held onto me and didn't say anything for a long time, I was more than content to hold her for as long as she needed me to, gently stroking her curls and enjoying the fresh scent of soap on her skin. Finally she pulled back and looked directly into my eyes, no longer showing sadness in hers, but a fire and determination that sent warning signals to my brain.

"You said you probably wouldn't get out of the truck, right?"

"Ramona."

"Well, then if the danger is that minimal, I can go with you."

"No, Ramona."

"It wasn't a request, Devaughn," she replied, spinning and going into the closet. She emerged dressed almost identically to me in some tight blue jeans, a black T-shirt, and her baby blue and navy blue Air Force Ones.

"Ramona."

"I'm not going to hear that shit, Dee. I'm going."

One thing I knew about her was that her determination and temper went hand-in-hand, and there was an iron will behind both. The only way I could see to keep her ass in the safety of the house was to keep shit all the way funky with her.

"Somebody's gonna die tonight."

"Huh?" she asked, stopping right in front of me.

"The nigga who is responsible for the two lovely bullet wounds I got is gonna die tonight. I'm gonna be the one to kill him."

Her mouth opened, but no words came out, just a grunt. Slowly she sat down on the bed and stared at the wall like it had the answers to what I knew had to be hundreds of questions. I didn't want to tell her, but at the same time part of me was glad it was out in the open. Now I had to hope she could deal with it.

"Babe?"

"Huh?"

"You okay?"

"Uh-huh."

"Say something, Ramona."

When she looked at me, her stare was blank and far away, like she was remembering me in the hospital or something. What she did next fucked me up completely. Suddenly her focus snapped back, and I could see that fire I loved burning bright again in her eyes.

"I'm going." She picked up the Taurus 9mm, checked the clip, and slid it in the back of her jeans like it was the most natural thing in the world.

"Huh?"

"You heard me, so let's go."

"Wait, wait, wait. Hold on a damn minute. What do you know about guns?"

"Sweetheart, I'm not just half Italian. I'm half Sicilian."

"So, are you saying my in-laws are—"

"Don't worry, Papi, you're gonna fit in just fine." She stood up to kiss me. All I could do was shake my head and pick up my own gun.

"You're sure?

"As sure as when I said 'I do' yesterday."

"Alright, let's go." I picked up the money and grabbing her hand as we walked to the elevator.

Keyz, Deshana, and Candy were in the kitchen when we walked in, and the conversation must have been about us, because it stopped as soon as we came in.

"Hey, Dad." She hugged me.

"Lil' M."

"Hi Ramona."

"Hi Deshana."

"Damn, what happened to your voice?"

My laughter earned me a sharp elbow from my wife and a look of hatred from Candy.

"I'm, um, coming down with something, I think."

"Oh. Okay. So what's the deal, old man?"

"Did your aunt brief you on the situation?"

"Somewhat, but she told me you would tell me everything."

"I will. Deshana, did you put everything I asked for in the room?"

"Yeah."

"Alright. Eternity, get the truck so we can go."

"Where are we going?" Candy asked.

"We're about to—"

"Deshana, you and Ramona go with Eternity, and I'll meet y'all outside in a minute."

"But, Dad—"

"Come on, Deshana," Ramona said, taking the money, her arm, and following Eternity out of the front door.

"You know I'm not gonna let you put yourself or the baby in danger."

"Let me? Nigga I'm grown, so I don't need your permission, do I?"

"Yeah, you do, because that's my baby you're carrying."

"Correction, this is my baby and my body, and you don't have jurisdiction over either. Besides, who's gonna be your backup? Ramona? What happens if she breaks a nail?"

She was asking for a fight, and I felt that all-too-familiar heat spreading throughout my body rapidly. She knew she was trying my patience, but I didn't see what she hoped to gain by pissing me off.

"What's wrong with you?"

"You know what's wrong with me. Don't ask dumb questions."

"Candy, listen, stop acting like I don't or I'm not supposed to care about you, because you know I do, and that won't stop. I never meant to hurt you, and you know that, so why are you acting like my intentions were to hurt you?"

"Weren't they?"

"Candy, we both went into this with our eyes wide open. I never expected us to love each other. I mean, you're wonderful. So no, I didn't want to use you, but I should've thought about how us having sex would play out."

"Dee, it hurts."

"Baby, listen." I stepped to her and took her face in my hands. "You're an amazing, sexy, intelligent woman, and deep down you know what? Don't let a nigga like me turn you cynical and bitter when you have so much to offer this world."

"Dee, I don't care about what I can offer someone else. I want you."

Her kiss took me by surprise, and in an instant I was wrapped in her arms, sucked in by the hot passion that always ignited us. She kissed me with her heart and soul, showing me the love she felt and I didn't deny. My body took over where my mind screamed stop, and before I knew it I had her suspended in the air up against the wall. The skirt she had on made for easy access, and I ripped her panties off, unzipped my pants, and slid my dick into her warm and waiting pussy before she realized what happened.

"Dee," she moaned when I lifter up into her, pinning her to the wall with my powerful strokes.

"Oh yes, fuck me Dee. God, mmm. I need you."

It wasn't making love. We were playing with fire, and I was lost in the moment, slamming into her so hard I could hear my balls slapping against her. I let her come off the wall, bent her over, grabbed her dreds, and pushed my way back inside her with such force her knees almost gave out. I rode her fast and hard, her pussy sounding off in smacking wet protest every time I dove deep inside her. It didn't take more than a few more strokes of my hard dick when I felt her cum, and then I went over the edge right behind her. No sooner had I stopped shaking with my orgasm when I heard the horn of my truck sound off loudly, scaring the shit out of me. Pulling out of her, I grabbed some paper towels, but before I could clean myself off, she was on her knees, licking and sucking me clean. I wiped the sweat off of my face and pulled her to her feet.

"You can't tell anyone."

"Will we keep doing it?"

Even though the words were only a whisper, the threat was clear. My answer was a firm kiss on her lips, and then I walked away, heading toward the front door.

"Devaughn."

"Yeah?"

"Be safe."

"Always," I told her, opening the door and taking a deep breath before walking toward the idling truck. I prayed I didn't smell like sex, but I need not worried, because when I opened the door, a cloud of smoke came out like the backseat was on fire.

"What took so long?" Deshana asked, coughing and passing me a blunt. I lit it before I answered, looking at my wife only to find love and compassion looking back instead of the suspicion I'd expected, making me feel something that was foreign: guilt.

"I'ma tell you something, Deshana, but you can't tell nobody, that includes your sisters."

"Okay, this sounds serious."

"It is. Candy is six weeks pregnant."

"Okay so— No way! Dad, you ain't been home but six weeks. Damn! You mean to tell me you was fucking that bitch raw? Are you fucking crazy?"

"Check your tone."

"My tone? Dad, do you understand what you just said? You just got married yesterday, and now you telling me that you got a baby on the way by someone else. Come on, you've gotta see how crazy this shit is."

"Yeah, I do, but that's life, and I'm dealing with it."

"Yeah, you dealing with it, but no wonder Candy has been looking at Ramona with death on her face. Ramona, did you know before you got married?"

"Yes, I knew, but I've known for a while now how she feels about your dad."

"But what about how he feels about her?"

"Naturally he loves her. I mean, she's the mother of his child, but that doesn't take away from our love."

Deshana just looked at her, but it wasn't a look of contempt. Unless I missed the mark, it was a look of admiration I saw, until she looked back at me.

"Let me guess, aunty doesn't know, huh?"

I continued to smoke, letting my silence answer the question for me.

"Woah, Dad. You're really a smooth jackass."

"Say it again. Go ahead, say it a-goddamn-gain, Deshana Marie Mitchell, and see what I do to you."

"Dee." Ramona slid toward me and took my hand in hers. "She has a right to whatever emotions she's feeling right now. At the same time, Deshana, you shouldn't talk to your father like that."

We rode on, no one really talking. My mind was on the events that were about to unfold, hoping I hadn't made a huge mistake by letting Ramona come with us. I'd never forgive myself if anything happened to her. Picking up the cell phone, I dialed my homeboy's number and waited for him to answer.

"What up, Tonio?"

"Ain't shit, what's good. bro?"

"You already know. Look, I'm on my way down there, and I got that for you. Where you wanna meet?"

"Do you know how to get to Park Place?"

"I can find it."

"Alright, how long is it gonna take you to get down here?"

"I should be there in, like, an hour and a half, two at the most."

"That's what it is. I'ma send someone to pick up that package for you now."

"I appreciate it, my dude."

"It's nothing. I know you would do the same for me."

"I'll holla at you in a minute."

"No doubt."

Hanging up the phone, I lit a cigarette and thought of the different ways I was gonna hurt this nigga. Not only had he tried to kill me, but also my daughter and my unborn child. Without question, he deserved everything that was coming to him. I quickly dialed another number and told my niggas where we were meeting so they could get there early. I didn't need any surprises.

"Dad?"

"Yeah?"

"You still mad at me?"

"A little."

"Don't be mad at me, Daddy." She climbed into my lap like she use to do during her visits to see me.

"You hurt my feelings."

"I'm sorry, Dad, really. I was surprised. I mean, you just came home, and with all the shit that's been going on, you haven't got to spend time with us. Now you've got a new baby on the way, and a wife."

"Sweetheart, I'm never gonna not have time for my divas, no matter who I'm with or who's pregnant or who's trying to kill me. Come on, you know better. Plus I'm gonna need all the help I can get. It's been ages since I had a newborn. Did you forget that you're the baby?"

"But I won't be anymore," she said sullenly.

I tilted her face until I was looking deeply into her eyes. "You'll always be my baby, Lil' M, don't ever doubt that. I love you."

"I love you too, Daddy. Hey, Ramona?"

"Huh?"

"For what it's worth, I think my grandma was right."

"Thanks."

We stayed just like that, in a cocoon of happiness with me holding my little girl and holding my wife's hand for the rest of the trip to Norfolk. When I looked at everything I had, I felt my soul settle just a little as some of the restlessness seeped away. After so much pain, it was humbling to know that I was still deserving of joy, and whatever higher power that existed beyond the stars felt the need to give its blessing.

"Dee, where are we going?"

"Park Place. You should see our team when we get out there. Hop up, Lil' M, let's get down to business."

"Alright, so what's the plan?"

"We're about to scoop up that nigga who left me for dead and take him to the play room."

"So what's the money for?"

"You gotta pay for what you want, baby girl. Don't trip, it ain't but 300."

"300? $300,000? Devaughn, you can't be serious," Ramona interrupted, wide-eyed.

"Chill, babe, it's all good."

"All good? Do I even wanna know how much you are willing to pay?"

"Probably not, but it's worth it to save my life and the lives of those that I love."

"So, Dad, What do you want me to do?"

I hit the button for the seat to come up and pulled out the HK and the Uzi, handing both of them to her and grabbed two extra clips. "I want you to do what you do best, only this time when we step out you'll be holding both of them. Eternity, you're back on duty with the baby, okay?"

"No problem."

"And listen, after tonight we're dumping all dirty guns, and I'll get new ones tomorrow."

"What do you need me to do?"

"Ramona, you're not doing shit except staying out of sight. Don't start trippin', I let you come, but there's no way in hell you're getting out of the truck!"

"He's right, Ramona. Not saying you can't take care of yourself, but everyone knows you're a P.O., so that's not going over real good in the projects."

I could imagine she wanted to argue, but only a fool would go against sound logic, so she kept her mouth shut and gave both of us angry looks instead.

"Dee, we're here."

"Everybody ready?" I pulled out my pistol to make sure everything was in good working order, opened the door, and me and Deshana stepped out into the cool evening air. I saw my soldiers everywhere, but they blended in so well with the neighborhood that I doubted Tonio knew he was surrounded. I spotted him immediately, leaning up against a hatchback coupe with two thick, dark-skinned females beside him. Deshana shut the door and chambered a bullet into the HK, smiling at the sound that echoed across the projects.

"Come on." I walked straight toward Tonio, but scanned everything around for signs of a threat.

"Muthafuckin' Big!"

"My Rick, nigga, fuck, what's up, family?"

"You see what it is, living like Daddy Warbucks."

"Damn right! I don't know what's hittin' on more, this ride or these beautiful ladies you got with you."

"From where I'ma sitting, you ain't doing bad your muthafuckin' self. Got Pocahontas chauffeuring you around, no shit. We came a long way, huh?"

"And I ain't got no rearview mirror."

"I like that. But look, y'all can't be out here with your shit out in the open, so let's handle this business."

"I'm with it."

He raised his hand in the air and a van came creeping out of the cut, stopping right next to my truck.

"Lil' M, get the bag."

Without a word, she ran to the truck and was back with the money before I could blink. I took the bag and handed it to him. He didn't even look at it, he just passed it to the females who took it and got in the car.

"You got something for me?"

"Of course I got it."

"Well, do I get to see it, huh?"

"No question." Again he raised his hand, and the van door slid open with two niggas jumping out, holding a long duffle bag.

"Lil' M, open the trunk."

I watched him being put into the trunk while Eternity kept a steady gaze on everything and everyone. Once the task was complete, I turned back to Rick.

"Good lookin', my nigga."

"Like I said, ain't nothing you wouldn't have done for me. What are your plans for his territory?"

"A takeover of course, but it's more than enough for both of us. What you think, we split?"

"Sounds like a plan."

"Give me a week to get everything together and I'll make another trip down so we can go over details, or you can come my way, for real."

"I been meaning to visit chocolate city."

"Say no more. We gonna make it right, so keep your eyes open, my nigga."

"Likewise, bro."

Deshana and I made our way back to the ride, where I found a nervous Ramona smoking a cigarette and clutching the pistol so tight her knuckles were white.

"It's okay, babe, we're leaving."

"Uh-huh."

"Let's go, Eternity."

I could feel the tension coming off Ramona in waves. She kept looking back toward the trunk, but she didn't say anything. As we got on the highway, I rolled up a blunt half the size of my arm, pulled Ramona onto my lap, and held her close while we smoked. Slowly she began to loosen up, and finally the shivering stopped. But she still hadn't said a word, and that worried me more than the kidnapping.

"Baby, he had me shot, tried to have me killed, and sent killers to eliminate everyone I care about. What am I supposed to do?"

"I know, Dee. I know you're only doing what you think you have to."

"But?"

"But— I don't know. I'm new at this, so taking a human life isn't second nature."

"Are you forgetting that you were shot, too?"

"No, and I'm still angry as hell about that."

"Let me ask you something, and I give you my word on the love that I have for you that whatever you say is how it goes."

"Okay."

"Do you want me to let him go? Before you answer, know and understand that he will come after me until I'm dead. Then he's gonna kill everyone, including you, so retaliation doesn't happen. Now, you may think I'm asking you as unfair question, but if we're gonna be together, then you have to face reality, and the reality is that if I don't kill him, he's gonna kill me."

The look she gave me was one of anger, but I could tell I'd made my point and finally gotten her to understand she would lose me. Part of me wondered if she would be better of if I had kept my secret from her, kept her in the dark so she could keep what innocence she had left rather than be tarnished by what I'd chosen to submerge myself in. I was forced to lie in the bed I'd made, but I wouldn't force her.

"I— I understand."

"You understand, but are you sure? Sweetheart, the life I lead is the life I chose, and it doesn't matter what circumstances were, because it was still my choice. I love you, but I can't choose this life for you. I understand all too well that sometimes love ain't enough."

She searched my face intently, looking for I-don't-know-what, but whatever it was, she must have found it. Her kiss was soft, but urgent and thorough enough to start that yearning inside me that was especially for her.

"I'm not giving you up for anyone or anything," she whispered seductively into my ear, nibbling gently on it and moving on to explore other parts of me with her tongue.

I signaled for Deshana to get in the front with Eternity and close the partition, tucking us deep into our hideaway. Taking the gun from her hand, I tossed it on the seat and unbuttoned her pants, dragging them down her legs hurriedly. I could feel her sucking on my neck as I spun her around until she was straddling me. Unzipping my pants, I guided her home swiftly, relishing the sound of her sharp intake of breath. Cupping her ass, I lifted her and brought her back down, slowly this time, seeking and finding her mouth with my own, catching my name on her lips. And then all hell broke loose.

"Dad, we got a big problem." Deshana started to slide the partition down to talk to us, causing me to lift Ramona off of me.

"What is it?"

"Cops."

"What?"

"Right behind us, and we're not out of Norfolk yet."

"How the fuck can they pull us over? We've got diplomatic plates!"

"I don't know. What do you want to do?"

The look on Ramona's face was one of sheer terror. Not only did we have a lot of dirty, illegal firepower, we had a fucking body in the trunk!

"Put your pants on. Eternity, Keyz said this muthafucka is tricked out. Do you know how to handle it?"

"Yeah, but I don't think we can outrun them, Dee. Not in this big-ass truck."

My mind was racing, but I was coming up empty. I couldn't think of one damn thing to get us out of what would soon be a disaster.

"Pull over."

"You sure, Dad?"

"Yeah, we got diplomatic plates, so any search of the truck is illegal."

"That's right," Ramona tuned in, already dressed and stashing shit in the hidden compartment. "Pass me your guns back here."

The window came down and the baby Uzi, HK, and .35mm came over the seat.

"Deshana."

"Huh?"

"All the guns."

I heard her suck her teeth as she tossed the .44 and the glock, too. Everything went into hiding except for my gun. I couldn't part with it because the situation felt all wrong as we slowed to a stop on the shoulder of the highway. We waited for the routine cop with his routine traffic questions.

"Say what?"

"It's the two cops from the hospital, and they're coming up one on each side with their guns drawn."

"Shit, they must work for Skino."

"Just stay cool." I pulled the .45 from behind me.

"Ramona, I want you to lay down on the floor and don't move."

"Dee?"

"It's okay, I'm not gonna let anything happen to you." I quickly opened the compartment back up and grabbed the .44, tossing it back to Deshana. I knew the cops couldn't see inside the truck, but they had just reached the bumper, meaning I had to move fast.

"Put the window up. Lil' M, wait for my signal."

A few seconds went by, and then I heard the sound of a gun barrel tapping the driver's side window.

"What seems to be the problem, officer?" Eternity asked.

"The problem is that this vehicle was identified in having been involved in a felony tonight. I'm gonna have to ask you and any other occupants to step out now."

My guess was correct. These boys were on the payroll. Ramona looked at me with tears in her eyes, somehow knowing the same thing I did.

"Stay down," I whispered, and she nodded that she understood.

"Step out of the vehicle for what, officer?"

"So that we can search it."

"I'm sorry, but you must not have noticed the diplomatic plates."

"I don't give a fuck about no diplomatic plates. Get the fuck out of the truck!"

I heard the door open, and I saw both women being pulled from the truck, but the cops made a terrible mistake. They didn't search them.

"Mitchell, we know you're in the back there. Exit the car slowly with your hands where we can see them!"

"I love you, Mona," I told her, opening the door, carefully concealing the pistol behind my leg. One cop was standing in front of Deshana, but the one on my side was standing near the driver's door, and he couldn't see me clearly.

"How you doing, detective?"

"Just fine. Obviously better than you."

"Maybe, but that all depends on how the lawsuit I'm gonna file will affect you."

"I don't give a fuck about a lawsuit, nigga."

"Oh. Suppose that means you're only interested in Skino?" The narrowing of his eyes told me I'd hit the nail on the head, which only meant one thing, and it wasn't good. "Yo, pop the trunk."

The cop did exactly what I thought he would do, which was turn his attention back on the women he had all but forgotten, and he paid for that with his life. The .45 screamed when I let loose with a double tap that severed half his head. Before he dropped, I heard two shots from the other side of the truck, and then Deshana was running toward me.

"Help me put the bodies in the trunk of their car." I was already dragging one to the back of the all-black Crown Victoria. We got them in with only two cars passing, but it was dark, so the odds were good that everything went unnoticed.

"Get their guns, too."

I opened the back door of the truck to find Ramona curled in a ball still on the floor, crying.

"Deshana, I need you to ride in the back with her and do what you can to keep her calm. E, I'm following you in the cop car. I want you to haul ass, understand?"

"I got it."

"Let's go."

I ran back to the Crown Vic, hopping in just in time to hear a report go out about suspicious behavior on the side of Highway 81. Shit was about to go from bad to worse if we didn't get the fuck outta Dodge. I laid rubber for a quarter mile when we pulled off, constantly checking the rearview mirror and listening to the police radio for signs of pursuit. I couldn't believe how fast shit had gotten out of hand. I was only supposed to come and pick a nigga up, and now I was racing home with two dead cops in the trunk and a wife who was damn near catatonic. This shit was unbelievable. I didn't know why I hadn't trusted my gut when the cops first showed up in my room acting fidgety, because I knew that something was wrong. My mind played out a million different scenarios, and the miles passed by until finally I saw the familiar safe haven of the house looming in the distance. Releasing a breath I hadn't realized I was holding, I guided the car to a stop behind my truck and got out, going straight to my wife. It was evident she was still shaken, but I could also see she was fucked up by the way she wobbled when her feet touched the ground.

"Deshana, what the hell?"

"You said to calm her down, so I did. I know whenever Mom gets the shakes all she has to do is take a few drinks and she's fine."

"That's because she's an alcoholic, fool! How much did she drink?"

"Half a bottle."

"Of?"

"Tequila."

"Oh, shit. Okay, come on, everybody in the house."

"Dee, I'm fine," she slurred before leaning against the truck and throwing up everything in her stomach. Tequila worked better than prune juice when it came to cleaning out the system, and the stench of it coming back up had me ready to join her. Everybody stepped back and gave her time to let it out, lighting cigarettes to cover the smell and calm the nerves.

"You okay, baby?"

"Uh-huh. I feel better now. It's probably a good idea if I lay down."

"I couldn't agree with you more. Eternity, Deshana, please get her upstairs and into bed. I'ma take care of the other situation."

"Alright, Dad, I'll meet you downstairs."

"I love you, Dee. No matter what."

"I love you too, Mona, now go get some rest."

While they escorted her to the house, I popped the trunk to find my guest was awake and struggling hard to get free. Making sure to bang his head on everything in the trunk, I dropped him on the ground and kicked him a few times. I could hear him mumbling obscenities behind the gag in his mouth, but I just laughed, slung him over my shoulder, and carried him into the house. It was as quiet as a cemetery when I came in, which was surprising since it wasn't even 1:00 a.m. yet. I hadn't expected Candy and Keyz to go to bed so early, especially with them knowing I was bringing this nigga back. It didn't matter, though, because the pleasure of killing him was all mine anyway. We took the elevator to the private torture chamber where Keyz had a metal table set up directly over a drain in the floor. Throwing him on the table, I pulled him out of the bag and stripped him of his blindfold. I was sated, smiling at the look of shock and fear.

"How's it going, big homie?" I asked, removing his gag and then the rest of his clothing.

"What the fuck are you doing, fool? You can't kill me!"

"Oh really? And why not?"

"Because I'm your direct superior, nigga. Now untie me and let me off this cold-ass table."

"I'm afraid it ain't going down like that, slim. See, you didn't just try to kill me, you went after my family. And for what? Because I killed a disrespectful-ass nigga who didn't know when to keep his mouth shut? Was that nigga's life worth yours?"

"You were out of line, little homie, and the shit you were doing was bringing too much heat. Ya know how the game goes."

"How the game goes? You stupid muthafucka, my team put together an offense that's bringing in half a billion dollars a year. I had the good sense and foresight to know who would benefit this nigga all those years ago! But somehow that's been overlooked because I murdered some niggas who needed it? You know what I

Aryanna

think? I think you didn't want to share the spoils, right? You ain't got to worry about that, though maybe you'll be a dog in the afterlife."

"You kill me and the nation will be gone, and everything you love, muthafucka. It's your decision."

The door opened behind me, stopping my retort as I turned to see Keyz, Candy, and Deshana come into the room, each with a variation of blank stares.

"What's going on?"

"Nothing, Big Head, but I had to be here for this. Hey, Skino."

"Fuck you, bitch!"

"Now, that's not very nice. May I?" she asked, pulling her pistol and stepping up to the table.

"Be my guest, just don't kill him yet."

While she went about pistol whipping him mercilessly, I went to Candy. "What have you been doing?" I asked in a harsh whisper.

"Dee, I think she knows."

"How the fuck is that possible?"

"I don't know. She— She's just been acting funny. Tara came in. She didn't say shit, but I could tell at the very least she heard me."

"You think she told Keyz?"

"I think anything is possible."

"Hey, Dee, I'm having all the fun. You better come on back before I kill this nigga."

I looked around to see her arms covered in blood and big spots of it on her clothes. His face was ruined, and he was barely conscious. The sound of him gargling blood and teeth was the only sound in the room. She had damn-near taken all the skin off of his forehead, and I could see it hanging off of her gun barrel. None of this disturbed me. The look in her eyes did.

"Keyz?"

"Huh?"

"What's up, sis?"

"What do you mean? Are you gonna finish this nigga or not?"

"Yeah, yeah, I'ma get to that, but what's going on with you? As far as I know, you never get your hands dirty. So what's really wrong?"

"Nothing's wrong, my nigga, I just wanted to be fucking this sorry-ass nigga up. Something wrong with that?"

It was the look, the far-off look, that was wrong. Even when she swore to me that everyone who had anything to do with me being shot had to die, her eyes still held life. Now they didn't. I only saw death. I saw absolutely nothing.

"Nah, ain't nothing wrong with that. I'ma leave that nigga until the morning. I wanna make sure he's conscious when I take the blowtorch to him."

"Ain't no need to wait. Let's kill this nigga now." She attacked him again with her pistol, laughing when he moaned and begged her to stop. I turned back to Candy and Deshana.

"Go wake Tara up, and I don't give a fuck if you gotta damn near kill her, just find out what she told Keyz. If she said anything about Candy and me, kill her."

"Are you sure, Dad?"

"Slit her throat!"

"Alright."

"Uh, bruh, you faking or getting on to killing this nigga?"

"I's coming now. Grab the torch. Candy, just stay out of the way."

She mouthed the words *I love you* and moved to sit in one of the chairs against the wall. Setting my mind back to the task at hand, I took the blowtorch from Keyz's outstretched hands and lit it. One of his eyes was still open, and when he saw it, tears began to fall to match the wails of sorrow coming from his swollen, bloody mouth.

"Come on, homie, don't do me like this. I gave you life, my nigga. You know this is deeper than banging with me and you. I swear if you let me live, we'll call a truce in front of the whole counsel."

"They wanted a truce, but you didn't take it, remember?"

"Nah, it wasn't even like that, bro. Listen to me."

His pleas fell on deaf ears, because I was done listening. I put the torch to the bottom of his right foot, and then all I heard were his agonizing screams of unspeakable pain. Not wanting to let him blackout, I kept moving the torch up and up his legs. When I got to his dick, he did black out, and I had to stop and wait for him to come back around. It didn't bother me, but by then I was so engrossed in inflicting pain on him I hadn't noticed my daughter's return. One look at her told me all I needed to know. She had blood caked under her fingernails, which meant Keyz knew I'd fucked Candy today. I wasn't in a hurry to deal with that, and thankfully my victim came back around.

"Dee. Devaughn. I've got money. Lots of money. You— You can have it. Please."

I looked down at the one eye pleading so desperately for his pathetic life, and for the first time I felt remorse for what I was doing. There used to be a time when I'd loved this nigga like a brother, we were loyal beyond reason. And there was a time I couldn't have imagined him trying to kill me. Times changed.

"You're my favorite EMU," I told him, kissing his bloody cheek, then I stuck the blowtorch into his eye socket and listened while he screamed his way to whatever awaited him beyond this world. The silence that followed was heavy. I turned to find Deshana shaking and smoking a cigarette, but Candy and Keyz were simply staring at me or through me. I couldn't tell which.

"What time is it, K?"

"A little after 2:00 a.m."

"Alright, we'll dump his body — and the cops, too — later today. Everybody should probably get some much-needed sleep."

"Dee, we need to talk."

"We can do it in the morning, K."

"No. No, we need to talk now."

"Kiara, I'm tired, and I have to check on my wife, so—"

"You wasn't worried about your wife when you were fucking mine earlier today."

I'd expected her to yell or scream, but she spoke the words so quietly I almost missed them. I didn't like that the blank look was back and her gun was still in her hand.

"What the fuck are you talking about?"

"Why Dee? You got Ramona. Why did you have to fuck Candy again? Or I guess the better question is, did you ever stop fucking her?"

Deshana bowed her head, and I could see the quiet tears sliding down Candy's face while her eyes shone with love and loss. The web of lies was coming undone, and all that could be left was aching pain and devastation.

"Kiara, I'm sorry. I never meant to hurt you, I swear. We didn't plan to love one another."

"No you didn't, so I guess that's my fault, huh? Ain't that what you said, Devaughn, that I should've known the outcome of you sleeping together? How could I, Dee? I trusted you."

Her words cut sharper than anything I'd known, and the truth of them wouldn't allow me to go on making excuses. I couldn't lay all the blame on her because Candy and I had played the major roles, continuing the betrayal. "I'm so sorry, Kiara. I'm so sorry, and you have to know that."

"Are you, Dee? Are you really?"

"Yes."

"What about you, Candy?"

"I'm—"

Keyz didn't let her finish as she backhanded her viciously, grabbing the pistol from her waist when she fell backward into the wall. Everything happened so fast that by the time it registered what was about to go down, I'd barely pulled my pistol out.

"Kiara! Don't! She's pregnant."

The room went still. I could tell Deshana was lost, unsure of what to do. Out of the corner of my eye, I saw her slowly reaching for her pistol, but Kiara knew what was coming. Quick as a cat, she had one trained on me and the other to the back of Candy's head.

"Reach for that gun, little girl, and Daddy or your little brother or sister goes bye-bye. It's your choice."

I shook my head once to let her know not to do it.

"Big brother, why are you pointing your gun at me? This domestic dispute is between me and this lying, cheating-ass bitch here."

"I just told you she's pregnant, now put the gun down before you accidently shoot her."

"Oh, trust me, my nigga, when I shoot this bitch, it ain't gonna be no type of accident."

"Come on, Keyz. Don't do this. You know I love you. Please don't make me choose."

"Choose? Nigga, you chose when you kept fucking the ungrateful-ass whore!"

"You're my sister, and I love you."

"But you love your babymama too, right? Why you so quiet, Candy? Tell your babydaddy how much you love him."

"Kiara."

"Talk, bitch!"

"I love you, Dee."

"Now, I love you, too."

"Aww, now ain't that sweet. Deshana, if you fidget one more motherfucking time, it's gonna be poppin'!"

"Come on, K. What the fuck do you want me to do?"

"Let me ask you something, Dee. You love all your babymamas, right?"

"You know I do."

"Equally, unless I'm in love with them. Do you love me, Dee?" she asked softly, her voice breaking slightly.

"You're my favorite person, my best friend. You know I love you. More than all the words in all the books in all the world."

She was crying now, big crocodile tears moving like missiles down her beautiful face.

"Yes. You know I love you. Why do you even have to ask me that?"

"I just wanna know who you love more, but before you answer, let me tell you something: I knew she was pregnant."

"What? How?"

"About two weeks ago she quit smoking and drinking. Then she began avoiding me. The truth came out when we had that foursome, because I know her pussy like I know my own."

"Why didn't you say something?"

"Why? Because I had a secret of my own. I'm pregnant, Dee."

I heard the words, and I was actually happy for her, but inside something didn't feel right. Now this situation didn't make any sense.

"Congratulations, but Keyz, how can you be mad at us if you were creeping your damn self?"

"You know, Candy and I have been together for going on twelve years now. In all that time, she's never been with a man. Even when I would have a little fling or something, she never did. So it didn't make sense to me that any dick could have her that open. I had to find out for myself."

"Okay, you admit that you did. Why can't we call it even and move on?"

"Because I understand now what it was that forced her to go back, even after you both promised. I understand the yearning, even now."

"Then it sounds like you two need to go your separate ways or be content to have your niggas on the side. Either way, we can stop this bullshit and put our guns away."

For a moment she just stared at me, and then she gave me the saddest smile I'd ever seen.

"You don't get it, Dee. You're the father of both of the babies."

"Have you lost your goddamn mind completely? Kiara, I love you, yes, but I'm the uncle to your baby, not its daddy."

"The child inside of me is yours, and—"

"Bitch, you done went loco! On what planet were me and you fucking?"

The transition was rapid, but I still caught it as her smile went from sad to malicious.

"Think back, Dee. Remember that night you found me sitting on your bed, crying?"

"Okay, I talked to you, held you, and sent your ass back to your room. I've been around a while. I know that babies ain't made like that. Try again."

"What were you doing before that?"

"Sleep! What use would I be comatose at 4:00 a.m.?"

"Did you dream, Dee?"

"Yeah, I—" The force of the realization was like a fierce blow to the chin. Deep down, I knew the truth. Maybe I always had. There was no way for her to know about the dream, unless—

"You heard me talking in my sleep, and now you're trying to say that I fucked you."

"No, I'm saying I fucked you. I rode that dick good and hard and made you cum until you passed out. Would you like me to give you the details of it, like grabbing onto the bed and screaming? How about how I started off slowly with my hands on your chest and then grabbed both your shoulders when I finished you?"

"Dad?"

"Dee?"

I couldn't speak. It was like my brain had locked up on me completely and reduced me to an infant. I was able to register Deshana's look of disbelief, Candy's look of horror, and Kiara's look of long-awaited triumph. That was her game all this time. Now she was carrying my child as well.

"Why? Why, Kiara? I'm your—"

"I know. And now you're my baby's father."

"So why are you still pointing your gun at me?"

"I— I want you to answer the question now. Who do you love more?"

And that last, final piece of the puzzle slid into place. I was supposed to choose between the two of them, but that decision would cost two lives in the end. How could I make that call? I'd killed a lot of people, but I couldn't suffer either of these deaths on my conscience.

"Answer me, dammit!"

There was no sadness left in her eyes. They were filled with a crazed look that remained on me, so I had to answer the question and end the life we'd created out of love.

"Candy, I—"

I never got to finish my thought before I felt the searing burn and heard the familiar thunder of the bullets that lifted me off my feet. I pulled the trigger with no aim, dropping the gun, and it hit the ground as the taste of my own blood filled my mouth. I heard the scream, but I didn't know if they were mine or someone else's. Through my tears, I could just make out Deshana's face crouched over me, her expression of anguish telling me what her words couldn't formulate. I wanted to say something, wanted to pray, but

I did neither. In the end, all I could do was think the words I'd been trying to get out: *Candy, I'm sorry.*
And then the world went black.

To Be Continued...
A Gangster's Revenge 2
Coming Soon

Coming Soon From Lock Down Publications

RESTRAINING ORDER

By **CA$H & COFFEE**

GANGSTA CITY **II**

By **Teddy Duke**

A DANGEROUS LOVE **VII**

By **J Peach**

BLOOD OF A BOSS **III**

By **Askari**

THE KING CARTEL **III**

By **Frank Gresham**

NEVER TRUST A RATCHET BITCH

SILVER PLATTER HOE **III**

By **Reds Johnson**

THESE NIGGAS AIN'T LOYAL **III**

By **Nikki Tee**

BROOKLYN ON LOCK **III**

Aryanna

By **Sonovia Alexander**

THE STREETS BLEED MURDER **II**

By **Jerry Jackson**

CONFESSIONS OF A DOPEMAN'S DAUGHTER **II**

By **Rasstrina**

WHAT ABOUT US **II**

NEVER LOVE AGAIN

By **Kim Kaye**

A GANGSTER'S REVENGE **II**

By **Aryanna**

<u>**Available Now**</u>

LOVE KNOWS NO BOUNDARIES **I II & III**

By **Coffee**

SILVER PLATTER HOE **I & II**

HONEY DIPP **I & II**

CLOSED LEGS DON'T GET FED **I & II**

A Gangster's Revenge

A BITCH NAMED KARMA

By **Reds Johnson**

A DANGEROUS LOVE **I, II, III, IV, V, VI**

By **J Peach**

CUM FOR ME

An **LDP Erotica Collaboration**

THE KING CARTEL **I & II**

By **Frank Gresham**

BLOOD OF A BOSS **I & II**

By **Askari**

THE DEVIL WEARS TIMBS

BURY ME A G **I II & III**

By **Tranay Adams**

THESE NIGGAS AIN'T LOYAL **I & II**

By **Nikki Tee**

THE STREETS BLEED MURDER

By **Jerry Jackson**

Aryanna

DIRTY LICKS

By **Peter Mack**

THE ULTIMATE BETRAYAL

By **Phoenix**

BROOKLYN ON LOCK

By **Sonovia Alexander**

SLEEPING IN HEAVEN, WAKING IN HELL **I, II & III**

By **Forever Redd**

THE DEVIL WEARS TIMBS **I, II & III**

By **Tranay Adams**

DON'T FU#K WITH MY HEART **I & II**

By **Linnea**

BOSS'N UP **I & II**

By **Royal Nicole**

LOYALTY IS BLIND

By **Kenneth Chisholm**

<u>BOOKS BY LDP'S CEO, CA$H</u>

TRUST NO MAN

TRUST NO MAN 2

TRUST NO MAN 3

BONDED BY BLOOD

SHORTY GOT A THUG

A DIRTY SOUTH LOVE

THUGS CRY

THUGS CRY 2

TRUST NO BITCH

TRUST NO BITCH 2

TRUST NO BITCH 3

TIL MY CASKET DROPS

Coming Soon

TRUST NO BITCH (KIAM EYEZ' STORY)

THUGS CRY 3

Aryanna

BONDED BY BLOOD 2

RESTRANING ORDER

A Gangster's Revenge

Made in the USA
Monee, IL
19 October 2024